THE
Black Pearl
SCOTT O'DELL

THE
Black Pearl

SCOTT O'DELL

A Yearling Book

Published by
Bantam Doubleday Dell Books for Young Readers
a division of
Bantam Doubleday Dell Publishing Group, Inc.
1540 Broadway
New York, New York 10036

ISBN: 0-440-22028-9

Reprinted by arrangement with Houghton Mifflin Company

RL: 5.2

Printed in the United States of America

Previous Yearling Edition and Laurel-Leaf Edition

June 1996

10 9 8 7 6 5 4 3 2 1

OPM

In that day, the Lord shall
punish the piercing serpent . . .
and he shall slay the dragon
that is in the sea.

ISAIAH

1

Everyone who lives in our town of La Paz, or along the far coasts or among the high mountains of Baja California, has heard of the Manta Diablo. There are many who live in the great world outside who have heard of him also, I am told. But of these thousands only two have really seen him. And of the two, only one is alive—I, Ramón Salazar.

There are many people in the town of La Paz and in Baja California who *say* they have seen the Manta Diablo. Old men around the fires at night tell their grandsons of the meetings they have had with him. Mothers seek to frighten bad children by threatening to call from the deeps of the sea this fearsome giant.

I am now sixteen, but when I was younger and did things I should not have done, my own mother said to me solemnly, "Ramón, if you do this thing again I shall speak a word to the Manta Diablo."

She told me that he was larger than the largest ship in the harbor of La Paz. His eyes were the color of ambergris and shaped like a sickle moon and there were seven of them. He had seven rows of teeth in his mouth, each tooth as long as my father's Toledo knife. With these teeth he would snap my bones like sticks.

Mothers of my friends also threatened them with the Manta Diablo. He was a somewhat different monster from the one my mother knew, for he had more teeth or less or eyes shaped in a different way or only a single eye instead of seven.

My grandfather was the most learned man in our town. He could read and use a pen and recite long poems right out of his memory. He had seen the Manta Diablo several times both at night and in the daytime, so he said, and his descriptions were nearer the truth as I know it.

Yet, I say to you, that of all the old men and the mothers and even my grandfather, not one has been able to give a true picture of the Manta Diablo.

It is possible that if Father Linares were living today he could tell us the truth. For it was he who first saw him, more than a hundred years ago.

That was the time when the Manta Diablo was a thing with claws and a forked tongue. It roamed our land back and forth and where it went the crops would wither and die and the air was foul. It was then that Father Linares commanded it in the name of God to disappear into the sea and remain there, which it obediently did.

I do not know whether Father Linares saw it again or not, but I do know that while it lived there in the sea it lost the claws and forked tongue and the evil smell. It became the most beautiful creature I have ever seen. Yes, beautiful. And still it was the same evil thing that Father Linares banished from our land many years ago. This is strange.

It is strange also that long ago I did not believe in the Manta Diablo. When my mother would threaten me I would quietly laugh to myself. Maybe I did not laugh but surely I smiled, for how could such a monstrous creature be alive in the world? And if it were alive how could my mother know it so well that she could speak a word and summon it to her side?

My blood felt cold nonetheless, and my scalp tingled when she spoke because I liked to feel this way. I wanted to believe that the Manta Diablo was really alive somewhere and that he would come when she called. Then I could see him and count his eyes and teeth while my mother explained at the very last moment that I had promised to be good so she did not want him to snap my bones after all.

That was long ago. Now that I have seen the Manta Diablo and struggled with him during the whole of one night and part of a day, in the waters of our Vermilion Sea, along with Gaspar Ruiz, the Sevillano, I wonder that I ever doubted.

But before I speak about that time and the three of us there on the quiet sea in a struggle of death, before I tell what I know about the Manta Diablo, I must also tell about The Pearl of Heaven.

2

It seems now as if it were a long time ago, but it was only last summer, on a hot day in August, that I sat at the window and watched our pearlers make ready to sail.

My father is Blas Salazar and for many years he was the most famous dealer in pearls anywhere on the Vermilion Sea. His name was known in Guaymas and Mazatlán and Guadalajara, even as far away as the City of México, for the fine pearls he wrested from the sea.

Last July on my birthday he made me a partner in his business. It was a grand fiesta and people came from the town and from miles around to drink chocolate and eat pig roasted in a deep pit. The biggest part was at the beginning of the feast when my father brought forth a sign, which he had hidden until that moment, and nailed it over the door of the office. The sign said in tall gilt letters SALAZAR AND SON, and under this legend in small letters was the word *Pearls*.

My father beamed with pride. "Ramón," he said, pointing at the sign, "look! Now there are two Salazars to deal in pearls. Now they sell twice as many pearls as before and finer ones. They sell pearls in all the cities of the world, these Salazars!"

I looked at the sign and blinked my eyes and felt

like shouting. But at that moment my father said something that made me feel like a boy and not like a partner in the House of Salazar.

"Ramón," he said, "put down your cuffs."

I am not scrawny, yet I am small for my age and thin. My wrists are very thin and my father was ashamed of them. Being so big himself, he did not like to think that his son was puny nor that anyone else thought so.

Afterward my father took me into the office and showed me how to open the huge iron safe. He showed me the trays lined with black velvet and filled with pearls of all shapes and colors and sizes.

"Tomorrow," he said, "I will begin the education. First I will teach you how to use the scales with accuracy, for the weight of the pearl is very important. Then I will explain the many shapes, which is also very important. Last of all I will show you how to hold a pearl up to the light and tell just by looking at it whether it is of excellent quality or good quality or only poor. Then, by the time you are as old as I am, you will be the best pearl dealer in all of our country and you can teach your son everything I have taught you."

That was the happiest day of my life, that day four months ago, and yet it was not all happy. Besides the embarrassment when my father had said, "Ramón, pull down your cuffs," there was also a big fear that kept worrying me.

As my father explained everything I had to learn, I feared that not soon would I have a chance to sail with the fleet. For many years I had dreamed of the time when I would be old enough to go. When you are sixteen, my father had said, you can sail with me and I will teach you how to dive in the deep water.

Many times he had said this, and I had counted the
weeks until I would be sixteen. But now that I was
sixteen at last, I could not learn to dive for pearls until I learned many other things.

There is a small window in our office. It is only a
slit in the stone and set high in the wall, and it looks
more like an opening in a jail than a window. It was
built that way so that not the smallest thief can
squeeze through. Yet it gives a fine view of the beach
and the Bay of La Paz. Furthermore, the men who
work there on the beach opening the shells cannot tell
whether they are being watched or not, which sometimes is a good thing.

On this morning as I sat at my desk I could see
the five blue boats of our fleet riding at anchor. Water
casks and coils of rope and supplies lay on the beach
ready to be carried aboard. My father strode back
and forth, urging the men to hurry for he wanted to
catch the outgoing tide.

The tide would turn in less than three hours, but in
that time I hoped to examine all of the pearls that lay
on my desk. There were still nine of them to look at
and weigh and duly note in the ledger, so quickly I
set to work.

Under the desk, wrapped in a neat bundle, were
my singlet, cotton pants, and a long, sharp blade my
grandfather had once given me with which to fend off
sharks. I was ready to sail with the fleet if my father
would give his consent, and I had made up my mind
to ask him, whatever happened.

The largest of the pearls was as big as the end of
my thumb, but flat in shape and with several dimples
that could not be peeled away. I placed it on the
scales and found that it weighed just over thirty-five
grains. In my head I changed grains into carats and

set down on a fresh page of the ledger: 1 baroque button. Dull. Wt. 8.7 cts.

The second pearl was smooth and pear-shaped. I held it to the light and saw that it gave off a soft amber glow, whichever way it was turned. I set it on the scales and then wrote down in the ledger: 1 pear. Amber. Wt. 3.3 cts.

I had put the seventh pearl on the scales and was carefully setting the small copper weights to make them come to a proper balance when I heard my father's steps outside the office. My hand shook at the sound and one of the weights slipped from my fingers. A moment later the heavy iron door swung open.

My father was a tall man with skin turned a deep bronze color from the glare of the sea. He was very strong. Once I saw him take two men who were fighting and grasp them by the backs of their necks and lift them off the ground and bump their heads together.

He came across the room to where I sat at the desk on my high stool and glanced at the ledger.

"You work with much rapidity," he said. "Six pearls weighed and valued since I left this morning." He wiped his hands on the tail of his shirt and took a pearl from the tray. "For this one," he said, "what is your notation?"

"Round. Fair. Weight 3.5 carats," I answered.

He rolled the pearl around in the palm of his hand and then held it to the light.

"You call this one only fair?" he asked. "It is a gem for the king."

"For a poor king," I said. After four months of working with my father I had learned to speak my mind. "If you hold it closer to the light, you will see that it has a flaw, a muddy streak, about midway through."

He turned the pearl in his hand. "With a little care the flaw can be peeled away," he said.

"That, sir, I doubt."

My father smiled and placed the pearl back in the tray. "I doubt it also," he said and gave me a heavy pat on the back. "You are learning fast, Ramón. Soon you will know more than I do."

I took a long breath. This was not a good beginning for the request I wanted to make. It was not good at all, yet I must speak now, before my father left. In less than a hour the tide would turn and the fleet sail from the harbor.

"Sir," I began, "for a long time you have promised me that when I was sixteen I could go with you and learn how to dive for pearls. I would like to go today."

My father did not reply. He strode to the slit in the wall and peered out. From a shelf he took a spyglass and held it to one eye. He then put the spyglass down and cupped his hands and shouted through the slit.

"You, Ovando, leaning against the cask, send word to Martín, who leans against the tiller of the *Santa Teresa*, that there is much work to do and little time in which to do it."

My father waited, watching through the slit, until his message was sent forward by Ovando.

"If you go with the fleet," he said, "then all the male members of the Salazar family will be on the sea at once. What happens if a storm comes up and drowns the both of us? I will tell you. It is the end of Salazar and Son. It is the end of everything I have worked for."

"The sea is calm, sir," I answered.

"These words prove you a true landsman. The sea is calm today, but what of tomorrow? Tomorrow it may stand on end under the lash of a chubasco."

"It is still a week or two before the big wind comes."

"What of the sharks? What of the devilfish that can wring your neck as if it were the neck of a chicken? And the giant mantas by the dozens, all of them the size of one of our boats and twice as heavy? Tell me, what do you do with these?"

"I have the knife that grandfather gave me."

My father laughed and the sound bounded through the room like the roar of a bull.

"Is it a very sharp knife?" he asked scornfully.

"Yes, sir."

"Then with much luck you might cut off one of the eight arms of the devilfish, just before the other seven wrap around you and squeeze out your tongue and your life."

I took another breath and brought forth my best argument.

"If you allow me to go, sir, I shall stay on deck while the others dive. I shall be the one who pulls up the basket and minds the ropes."

I watched my father's face and saw that it had begun to soften.

"I can take the place of Goleta," I said quickly, to follow up the advantage I had gained. "There is an apology to make, sir. At noon Goleta's wife came to say that her husband is sick and cannot sail. I forgot to tell you."

My father walked to the iron door and opened it. He looked at the sky and at the glossy leaves of the laurel trees that hung quiet on their branches. He

closed the door and put the tray of pearls in the safe
and turned the bolt.

"Come," he said.

Quickly I picked up my bundle and in silence we
went into the street and up the winding path to the
church high on the bluff. My father always came here
before the fleet sailed to ask the protection of the
Madonna against the sea's dangers. And when the
fleet came home the first thing he did was to hurry
here and offer thanks for its safe return.

The church was deserted, but we found Father
Gallardo and aroused him from his afternoon siesta.
While he stood beside the Virgin and held his arms
outstretched in benediction we knelt and bowed our
heads.

"We ask Your mercy for these men," Father Gallardo said. "Give them good winds and good tides.
Guard them against the hazards of the deep waters,
make their journey fruitful in all ways, and bring
them back in health."

I glanced up at the Madonna as Father Gallardo
finished his benediction. She stood calmly in her
niche fashioned of seashells, dressed all in white velvet. She had the face of a child, but she was really a
young woman, neither Indian nor Spanish, with broad
Indian cheeks of a golden brown, and eyes of the
women of Castile, large and shaped like almonds.

I had always loved her, yet never so much as I did
at this moment. I was still gazing at her when my father gave me a pinch on the shoulder and motioned
me to follow.

We went outside and stood for a moment under the
laurel trees.

"I note the bundle under your arm," my father said,

"so you must have told your mother when you left this morning."

"I said nothing to her. But I shall go now to tell her that I am leaving."

"No, I will send someone with a message. If you go it will take time. We are already late. Besides, there will be tears and lamentations, which are poor heralds for a voyage."

He summoned a boy who was watching us from a distance and gave him a message to take to my mother. Then we went down the hill toward the beach. The sun was setting, yet I could clearly see the fine blue boats of our fleet riding at anchor. In the fading light they looked silver, like live silver fish floating there. Beyond them the harbor stretched away for leagues between the headlands to the island of Espíritu Santo and the open sea.

I wanted to ask my father many things as we went down the hill, but my head was buzzing with excitement and I could think of nothing to say.

3

There were five boats in our fleet. Each was about twenty feet long and broad-beamed, with a high prow and stern like a canoe, and a small square sail. They were built on the beach of our town, but the wood came from the mahogany forests of Mazatlán. Each was named after a saint and all were painted blue, the blue of the sea where the water is very deep.

Each boat carried four or five men. On our boat, the *Santa Teresa*, there were besides my father and myself an Indian and a young man named Gaspar Ruiz.

This Ruiz had come to our town about a month before from Seville in Spain, or so he said, and therefore we called him the Sevillano.

He was tall and his shoulders were so wide and powerful that they seemed to be armored in steel instead of muscle. His hair, which was gold-colored, grew thick on his head like a helmet. He had blue eyes, so blue and handsome that any girl would have envied them. His face was handsome, too, except that around his mouth there always lurked the shadow of a sneer.

Besides this, nowhere on the Vermilion Sea could you find a better diver for pearls than Gaspar Ruiz.

There were some who could stay under water for longer than two minutes, but to the Sevillano three minutes was an easy dive. And once when he had to hide from a large gray shark he was down four minutes and came up laughing.

Also he was a great braggart about the things he had done in Spain and elsewhere. Not only did he brag about these things, but many of them were tattooed on his body. There was a picture in red and green and black ink of Gaspar Ruiz fighting an octopus that had a dozen tentacles. Another showed him thrusting a long sword into a charging bull. Still another showed him choking a mountain lion to death with his bare hands.

These scenes were tattooed on his shoulders and arms and even on his legs, so that he looked very much like a picture gallery walking around.

We had not sailed far that night before the Sevillano began to talk about himself. He sat with his back against the mast and told a long story of how he had once dived in the Gulf of Persia and there found a pearl bigger than a hen's egg.

"What did you do with it?" my father asked.

"I sold it to the Shah."

"For much money?"

"Much," said the Sevillano. "So much that I bought a pearling fleet of my own. It was larger than yours. Today I would be a rich man if it had not foundered in a bad storm."

The Sevillano went on to tell about the storm, which must have been the greatest ever seen in the world, and how he saved his own life and the lives of his crew.

Before I became a partner with my father, sometimes I used to see him on the beach when the boats went out or when they came in and sometimes in the plaza. He always had a group around him, listening to his tales, but somehow I felt that he was talking to me more than to the others. Once when I questioned him in fun about one of these tales that I knew to be a lie, he turned on me.

"You do not believe that I tell the truth?" he said, clenching his teeth. Before I could answer, he said, "You are the son of a rich man and you live in a big house and you eat good food and all of your life you have done little. Nor will you ever do more."

Too surprised to speak, I was silent. He watched me for a moment and then took a step toward me and lowered his voice. "Your father is a rich man. My father was a poor man whose name I do not know. From the time I could walk I have done something and in my life I have done many things and what I have done I talk about truthfully. So guard your tongue, mate."

I mumbled an apology and walked away, but when he thought I was out of hearing I heard him say to his friend, "That one who just left us. Have you noticed the red hair that sticks up on his head like the comb of a rooster? Well, that comes from Africa. It is from the infidel blood of Moors and Berbers."

I was about to turn around and confront him. He was older than I and stronger and he carried a knife at his belt, but it was not this that held me back. I knew that my father would think it an insult to the Salazar name for me to start a brawl in a public place, no matter what the cause. So I swallowed my pride and I walked on as if I had not heard.

I said nothing to my father about this encounter, and afterward when I met the Sevillano I said nothing to him. I acted as if I did not remember what he

had said to me or what I had overheard. And when I
became a partner in the firm and he would come to
the office to get his pay, I acted no differently. Yet I
had not forgotten the encounter nor, I am sure, had
he.

On this night as we sailed out of the harbor and
he sat and told the tall tale about the storm and his
rescuing the whole crew of his pearling fleet, I felt
that he was talking to me more than to the others. I
felt that he was trying to goad me into saying something as I had before, so that he could make me
uncomfortable in front of my father. I therefore listened and kept silent.

We reached the pearling beds at dawn and anchored
the five boats in a cluster over a reef where the shells
grew.

Everything was new to me. I had heard many stories of the pearling beds since the time I was old
enough to listen, from my father and grandfather and
from my friends who were the sons of pearlers. But to
be really there on the sea with the sun coming up in a
coppery haze and watch the men slip out of the boats
into water clear as air, was to me a part of a long
dream come true.

My father showed me how to pull up the basket
when it was full and how to stack the shells in the
boat. Then he took the sink stone in one hand, carefully coiled the rope that was attached to it and tied
to the boat, picked up the basket and its rope, and
went over the side. Down he went with the heavy
stone until he reached the bottom.

Through the clear water I watched him drop the
stone, take the big knife from his belt, and start to
pry the oyster shells from the rocks. When the basket
was full he gave a tug at the rope and I pulled it up.

A moment later he rose, trailing a stream of bubbles from his mouth, and I stacked the shells as I had been told and drew up the sink stone for the next dive.

The Sevillano had gone down before my father and was still down as he dived again. When the Sevillano came to the surface he held onto the side of the boat and glanced up at me.

"How does the work go?" he said.

"I learn."

"There is not much to learn, mate. You pull the shells up and then the sink stone and you stack the shells and then you wait a while and do it all over again. It is work for children."

He spoke softly and smiled, but I knew what he meant. "It would be fun to dive," I answered him.

"More fun, mate, but more danger too."

He pointed to the arm he was resting on the gunwale. From his elbow to wrist ran a long, jagged scar, as if the arm had been pulled through the jaws of a steel trap.

"This one," he said, "I got from a burro clam. I put my hand down deep into a crevice and snap, it was not a crevice but the mouth of a burro, the father of all burros. Señor Clam had me tight, but I did not leave my arm with him, as you can see. That was in the Gulf, yet there are many burros here in the Vermilion." He looked up at me again and smiled. "It is better, mate, that you stay in the boat."

The Indian who was working with the Sevillano handed him the sink stone and the Sevillano went down, saying nothing more to me. Nor did he speak to me again that morning. At midday the *Santa Teresa* was loaded with shells and low in the water, because the Sevillano did the work of three divers, so my father sent him out to help in the other boats.

From time to time during the afternoon, when he came up for air, he would call over to me, "Be careful, mate, and do not get your foot caught in the rope," or "There are sharks around, Señor Salazar, mind that you do not fall in the water."

Such things as that I heard during the whole of the afternoon. My father also heard them, though the Sevillano usually spoke to me when he thought my father was not listening.

"He is a troublemaker," my father said, "but let him talk. What do you care what he says? Remember that he is the best gatherer of pearls we have. And it is for pearls that we are here on the sea, not for other reasons."

By dark the boats were piled high with cargo and we set sail for La Paz. The moon came up and a brisk wind that filled the sails. The Sevillano was in good spirits, as if he had not made dozens of deep dives that day. He perched himself on the mound of shells and once more told how he had found the great pearl in the gulf of Persia, the same tale he had told before but longer. Again I had the feeling that his story was meant for me more than the others.

And as I listened to him a dream began to take shape in my mind. It was a fanciful dream that made me forget the insults that I had suffered silently. I saw myself in a boat anchored in a secret lagoon somewhere in the Vermilion Sea. I put a knife in my belt and grasped the basket and the heavy sink stone and plunged to the bottom. There were sharks swimming around me in slow circles, but I gave no heed to them. I pried clump after clump of shells from the rocks, filling my basket. After I had been down for three or four minutes, I floated to the surface through the circling sharks, and climbed into the boat and pulled up the basket. Then I pried open the shells, one after the other. Nothing. At last there was only one shell left. Discouraged, I opened it and was about to toss it away when I saw before me a pearl larger than my fist that shone as if a fire burned inside . . .

Right at that moment, just as I was about to clutch the pearl in my hand, the Sevillano stopped talking. Suddenly he stood up on the mound and pointed astern, along the path the moon was making on the sea.

"Manta," he shouted, "Manta Diablo."

I jumped to my feet. I could see nothing at first. Then the boat rose on a wave and I made out a silvery shape swimming half out of the water not more than a furlong away.

Truthfully, I must say that for all its beauty the manta is a fearsome sight to those who sail our Vermilion Sea. There are small mantas, no larger when they are full grown than ten feet from one wing tip to the other. But there are some that measure twice that length and weigh most of three tons.

Both kinds are shaped very much like a giant bat and they swim through the water with a regular upward and downward beat of their flippers. And both have a mouth so enormous that a man may easily put his head into it and on either side of this maw are large lobes like arms, which the manta pushes out and then draws in to capture its prey.

Their prey surprisingly is not the shoals of fish that abound in our sea, but shrimp and crabs and such small things. Most of the mantas have a pilot fish that swims along beneath them. These fish swim in and out of their mouths, it is said, to clean up the pieces of food that catch in their plate-like teeth.

And yet for all of his friendly ways, the manta is a fearsome beast. When aroused by some careless insult, it can break a man's neck with a flick of its long tail or lift one flipper and wreck the strongest boat.

"Manta," the Sevillano shouted again. "El Manta Diablo!" His Indian helper quickly scrambled away and crouched down in the bow of the boat and began to mutter to himself.

"No," said my father, "it is not the Diablo. Him I have seen and he is bigger by twice than this one."

"Come where you can see better," said the Sevillano. "It is the Manta Diablo. I know him well."

I was certain that he was trying to scare the Indian and my father was certain of it, too, for he lashed the tiller and climbed to where the Sevillano stood. He glanced astern for a moment and then went back to the tiller.

"No," he said, loud enough for the Indian to hear, "it is not even the small sister of the Diablo."

The Indian fell silent, but he was still frightened. And as I watched the manta swimming along behind us, its outstretched fins like vast silvery wings, I remembered that once I had also been frightened at the very sound of the name.

At last the manta disappeared and near dawn we rounded El Magote, the lizard tongue of land that guards the harbor, and anchored our boats. As my father and I walked home in the moonlight, he said,

"About the Sevillano, let me repeat to you. Treat him with courtesy. Listen to his boasts as if you believed them. For he is a very dangerous young man. Only last week I learned from a friend who lives over in Culiacán that the Sevillano was born there. And that he has never been in Seville nor any part of Spain nor in the Gulf of Persia nor anywhere except here on the Vermilion. Also, that he has had many fights in Culiacán, one of them fatal."

I promised my father that I would obey him, but as we walked toward home I again thought of my dream and the big pearl I had found and how surprised the Sevillano would be when he saw it.

4

Four days passed and I was standing at the desk, with a pen over my ear and the leather-bound ledger open in front of me. I was watching a canoe that moved around the tip of the lizard tongue. It was a red canoe and came swiftly, so I knew it belonged to the Indian Soto Luzon.

I was glad to see old Luzon. He had sold pearls to my father for many years. He came about every three months and never brought more than one, but it always was a pearl of good quality. Soon after I began to work with my father he had brought in a beautiful pearl of more than two carats.

As I watched Luzon beach the canoe and come up the path, I hoped he was bringing another like it, for the yield from our last trip had been poor. Five boatloads of shells had yielded no round or pear-shaped pearls and only a handful of buttons and baroques, all of them dull.

I opened the door at his timid knock and invited him to come in and sit down.

"I have traveled all night," Luzon said. "If it pleases you, I would like to stand."

Luzon never sat. He had an Indian's thin legs but a powerful chest and thick arms that could wield a paddle for hours and not grow tired.

"I passed your boats this morning," he said. "They were near Maldonado."

"They are going to Isla Cerralvo."

The old man gave me a shrewd look. "The fishing is not good around here?"

"Good," I said. It was not wise to say that it was poor, when he had come to sell a pearl. "Very good."

"Then why, señor, do the boats go to Cerralvo?"

"Because my father wants to search there for the black ones."

The old man fumbled in his shirt and pulled out a knotted rag and untied it. "Here is a black one," he said.

I could see at a glance that it was round and of a good quality, like the pearl I had bought from him three months before. I placed it on the scales and balanced it against the small copper weights.

"Two and a half carats," I said.

My father never haggled with Luzon and always gave him a fair price and had told me to do the same. For that reason old Luzon always brought his pearls to Salazar and Son, although there were four other dealers in our town.

"Two hundred pesos," I said.

This sum was about fifty pesos more than my father would have offered, but a plan was taking shape in my mind and I needed the old man's help. I counted out the money and he put it in his shirt, probably thinking to himself that I was not so smart as my father.

"You always bring in good pearls. Black ones," I said. "There must be many in your lagoon. If you permit me I will come and dive there. All the pearls I find I will pay you for."

The old man looked puzzled. "But you are not a diver," he said.

"You can teach me, señor."

"I have heard your father say many times, since the time you were a child, that he did not raise you to drown in the sea or to give an arm or a leg to a burro shell."

"My father," I said, "has gone to Cerralvo and he will not return for a week or more."

"And your mother and your sister, what will they say?"

"They will say nothing because today they go to Loreto." I paused. "You will teach me to dive and I will look for the big one and when I find it I will pay you what it is worth."

"The big one I have searched for many years," Luzon said. "How is it found in a week?"

"You can find the big one in a single dive."

The old man pulled at his stubbly chin. He was thinking, I knew, about his wife and his two unmarried daughters and his three young sons, and all these mouths he had to feed every day.

"When do you wish to go?" he said.

"I wish to go now."

Luzon hitched up his frayed trousers. "After I buy a sack of frijoles and a sack of flour, then we go."

The old man left and I put the pearls away and locked the safe. I took the bundle from under the desk, my pants, a shirt, and the knife. I closed the door and locked it. As I walked down to the beach, I thought about the great pearl I had dreamed of while the Sevillano was bragging. I thought of how surprised he would be when he came back from Cerralvo and found the whole town of La Paz talking about the monster pearl Ramón Salazar had found.

It was a dream so wild that only a very young man and a stupid one could dream it. And yet, as happens sometimes, the dream came true.

5

The lagoon where the old man lived was about seven leagues from La Paz and we should have reached it by midnight. But the currents and the wind were against us, so it was near dawn before we sighted the two headlands that marked the lagoon's hidden entrance.

You could pass this entrance many times and think that it was only an opening in the rocks that led nowhere. As soon as you passed the rocks, however, you came to a narrow channel that wound like a snake between the two headlands for a half mile or farther.

The sun was just rising when the channel opened out and suddenly we were in a quiet oval-shaped lagoon. On both sides of the lagoon steep hills came down to the water and at the far end lay a shallow beach of black sand. Beyond were two scraggly trees and beneath them a cluster of huts where breakfast fires were burning.

It was a peaceful scene that lay before me, much like many other lagoons that dot our coast. But there was something about the place that made me feel uneasy. At first I thought it must be the barren hills that closed in upon the lagoon and the coppery haze that lay over it, and the beach of black sand and the quiet. I was soon to hear that it was something else, something far different from what I thought.

The old man paddled slowly across the lagoon, carefully raising and lowering the paddle, as if he did not want to disturb the water. And though he had talked most of the time before we reached the lagoon he now fell silent. A gray shark circled the canoe and disappeared. He pointed to it, but said nothing.

Nor did he speak again until we beached the canoe and were walking up the path to the huts. Then he said, "It is well to hold the tongue and not to talk needlessly when you are on the lagoon. Remember this when we go out to dive, for there is one who listens and is quickly angered."

Indians are superstitious about the moon and the sun and some animals and birds, especially the coyote and the owl. For this reason I was not surprised that he wished to warn me.

"Who is it that listens and grows angry?" I asked him.

Twice he glanced over his shoulder before he answered. "The Manta Diablo," he said.

"El Diablo?" I asked, holding back a smile. "He lives here in your lagoon?"

"In a cave," he answered, "a big one which you can see just as you leave the channel."

"The channel is very narrow," I said, "barely wide enough for a canoe. How does a giant like El Diablo swim through it? But perhaps he does not need to. Perhaps he stays here in your lagoon."

"No," the old man said. "He travels widely and is gone for many weeks at a time."

"Then he must swim through the channel somehow."

"Oh, no, that would be impossible, even for him.

There is another opening, a secret one, near the place where you enter the channel. When he swims out to sea, it is this one he uses."

We were nearing the huts clustered beneath the two scraggly trees. A band of children came running out to meet us and the old man said nothing more about El Diablo until we had eaten breakfast, slept the morning away, eaten again, and gone back to the lagoon.

As we floated the canoe and set off for the pearling reefs, the old man said, "When the mist goes, that means El Diablo has gone, too."

It was true that the red mist was gone and the water now shone green and clear. I still smiled to myself at the old man's belief in El Diablo, yet I felt a little of the excitement that I had felt long ago when my mother threatened me with the monster.

"Now that he is gone," I said, "we can talk."

"A little and with much care," Luzon replied, "for he has many friends in the lagoon."

"Friends?"

"Yes, the shark you saw this morning and many small fish. They are all friends and they listen and when he comes back they tell him everything, everything."

"When he leaves the lagoon, where does he go?"

"That I do not know. Some say that he takes the shape of an octopus and seeks out those pearlers who have done him a wrong or spoken ill of him. It is also said that he takes the shape of a human and goes into La Paz and seeks his enemies there in the streets and sometimes even in the church."

"I should think that you would fear for your life and leave the lagoon."

"No, I do not fear El Diablo. Nor did my father before me. Nor his father before him. For many years they had a pact with the Manta Diablo and now I keep this pact. I show him proper respect and tip my hat when I come into the lagoon and when I leave it. For this he allows me to dive for the black pearls which belong to him and which we now go to search for."

Silently the old man guided the canoe toward the south shore of the lagoon, and I asked no more questions for I felt that he had said all he wished to say about the Manta Diablo. In two fathoms of water, over a reef of black rocks, he dropped anchor and told me to do the same.

"Now I teach you to dive," he said. "First we start with the breathing."

The old man lifted his shoulders and began to take in great gulps of air, gulp after gulp, until his chest seemed twice its size. Then he let out the air with a long whoosh.

"This is called 'taking the wind,'" he said. "And because it is very important you must try it."

I obeyed his command, but filled my lungs in one breath.

"More," the old man said.

I took in another gulp of air.

"More," the old man said.

I tried again and then began to cough.

"For the first time it is good," the old man said. "But you must practice this much so you stretch the lungs. Now we go down together."

We both filled our lungs with air and slipped over the side of the canoe feet first, each of us holding a sink stone. The water was as warm as milk but clear so that I could see the wrinkled sand and the black rocks and fish swimming about.

When we reached the bottom the old man put a foot in the loop of the rope that held his sink stone and I did likewise with my stone. He placed his hand on my shoulder and took two steps to a crevice in a rock that was covered with trailing weeds. Then he took the knife from his belt and thrust it into the crevice. Instantly the crevice closed, not slowly but with a snap. The old man wrenched the knife free and took his foot out of the loop and motioned for me to do the same and we floated up to the canoe.

The old man held out the knife. "Note the scratches which the burro shell leaves," he said. "With a hand or a foot it is different. Once the burro has you he does not let go and thus you drown. Take care, therefore, where you step and where you place the hand."

We dived until night came, and the old man showed me how to walk carefully on the bottom, so as not to muddy the water, and how to use the knife to pry loose the oysters that grew in clumps and how to get the shells open and how to search them for pearls.

We gathered many baskets that afternoon but found nothing except a few baroques of little worth. And it was the same the next day and the next, and then on the fourth day, because the old man cut his hand on a shell, I went out on the lagoon alone.

It was on this day that I found the great Pearl of Heaven.

6

A red haze hung over the water as I floated the canoe on the morning of the fourth day and began to paddle toward the cave where the old man said the Manta Diablo lived.

The sun was up but the haze hung so thick that I had trouble locating the channel. After I found it I searched for almost an hour before I sighted the cave. It was hidden behind a rocky pinnacle and faced the rising sun, and the opening was about thirty feet wide and the height of a tall man, and curved downward like the upper lip of a mouth. I could not see into the cave because of the red mist, so I drifted back and forth and waited until the sun rose higher and the mist burned away.

I had talked to the old man the night before about the cave. We had eaten supper, and the women and children had gone to bed, and the two of us were sitting around the fire.

"You have fished everywhere in the lagoon," I said, "but not in the cave."

"No," he said. "Nor did my father nor his father."

"Big pearls may grow there."

The old man did not answer. He got up and put wood on the fire and sat down again.

"The great one itself, the Pearl of Heaven, may lie there," I said.

Still he did not answer, but suddenly he looked across the fire. It was a fleeting look that he gave me and yet its meaning was as clear as if he had spoken to me and said, "I cannot go to the cave to search for pearls. I cannot go because I fear the Manta Diablo. If you go there, then it is alone. El Diablo cannot blame me."

And that morning when I went down to the beach he did not go with me. "The wound on my hand hurts very much," he said, "so I will stay behind." And the look he gave me was the same I had seen the night before.

At last, about midmorning, the sun burned away the mist and I could see for a short distance into the cave. I paddled through the mouth and soon found myself in a vast vault-like room. The walls of the room were black and smooth and shone from the light that came in through the opening.

Near the mouth of the cave the water was very clear. I picked up my basket and sink stone, took a deep breath, and slipped over the side of the canoe, remembering all that the old man had taught me.

I reached the bottom after about a fathom and a half. I looped my foot in the rope tied to the sink stone and waited until the bubbles that had risen behind me disappeared and I could find the bed of shells I had noticed from above. The bed was five steps away toward the mouth of the cave. I walked carefully in the sand as I had learned to do.

The shells were the largest I had ever seen. They were half the length of my arm and thick through as my body and covered with weed that looked like a woman's hair. I chose the nearest one, which seemed to be easier to get at than the others. I took out my knife and worked quietly, but a school of small fish kept swimming in front of my eyes, so I failed to pry the shell loose before my lungs began to hurt and I had to go up.

On my second dive I had no sooner reached the bottom than a shadow fell across the bed where I was working. It was the shadow of a gray shark, one of the friendly ones, but by the time he had drifted away my breath was gone.

I dived six times more and worked quickly each time I went down, hacking away with my sharp knife at the base of the big shell where it was anchored to the rock. But it had been growing there for many years, since long before I was born, I suppose, and it would not come free from its home.

By this time it was late in the afternoon and the light was poor. Also my hands were bleeding and my eyes were half-blind with salt from the sea. But I sat in the canoe and thought of all the hours I had spent for nothing. And I thought too of the Sevillano and the great pearl he had found, or said he had found, in the Gulf of Persia.

I filled my lungs and took the sink stone and went down again. With the first stroke of my knife, the shell came free. It toppled over on one side, and I quickly untied the rope from the sink stone and looped it twice around the shell and swam back to the surface. I pulled up the shell, but it was too heavy for me to lift into the canoe, so I tied it to the stern and paddled out of the cave.

Across the lagoon I could see the old man standing among the trees. From time to time during the day I had caught glimpses of him standing there with his eyes fixed on the cave. I knew that I could drown and

he would not try to save me, and that he was telling
El Diablo all the while that he had not wanted me to
go to the cave and that he therefore was not to
blame. But I also felt that if I found a pearl he would
be willing to take his share because he had nothing to
do with finding it.

He came out from the trees as I paddled across the
lagoon and strolled down to the beach as if he did not
care whether I had found a pearl or not. I suppose
this was to show El Diablo and his friends the fish
and the long, gray shark that Soto Luzon was without
blame.

"A big one," he said when I dragged the shell
ashore. "In my life I have never seen such a monster.
It is the grandfather of all oysters that live in the sea."

"There are many in the cave bigger than this one,"
I said.

"If there are so many," he answered, "then the
Manta Diablo cannot be mad that you have taken
only one of them."

"Perhaps a little mad," I said and laughed, "but not
much."

The mouth of the oyster was closed and it was hard
to put my blade between the tight edges of the shell.

"Lend me your knife," I said. "Mine is blunted from
use."

The old man placed his hand on the hilt of his
knife and pulled it from the sheath and then slipped
it back again.

"I think it is better if you use your own knife," he
said and his voice began to tremble as he spoke.

I wrestled a long time with the oyster. At last the
hard lips began to give a little. Then I could feel the
knife sink through the heavy muscles that held them
together and suddenly the lips fell apart.

I put my finger under the frilled edge of the flesh as I had seen my father do. A pearl slid along my finger and I picked it out. It was about the size of a pea. When I felt again, another of the same size rolled out and then a third. I put them on the other half of the shell so they would not be scratched.

The old man came and leaned over me, as I knelt there in the sand, and held his breath.

Slowly I slid my hand under the heavy tongue of the oyster. I felt a hard lump, so monstrous in size that it could not be a pearl. I took hold of it and pulled it from the flesh and got to my feet and held it to the sun, thinking that I must be holding a rock that the oyster had swallowed somehow.

It was round and smooth and the color of smoke. It filled my cupped hand. Then the sun's light struck deep into the thing and moved in silver swirls and I knew that it was not a rock that I held but a pearl, the great Pearl of Heaven.

"Madre de Dios," the old man whispered.

I stood there and could not move or talk. The old man kept whispering over and over, "Madre de Dios."

Darkness fell. I tore off the tail of my shirt and wrapped the pearl in it.

"Half of this is yours," I told him.

I handed the pearl to him, but he drew back in fear.

"You wish me to keep it until we reach La Paz?" I said.

"Yes, it is better that you keep it."

"When shall we go?"

"Soon," he said hoarsely. "El Diablo is away but he will come back. And his friends will tell him then about the pearl."

7

We did not wait to eat supper. While I dragged the
canoe into the water, the old man went up to the huts
and came back with a handful of corn cakes. As we
passed the cave, he touched his hat and mumbled
something to himself, then dug his paddle into the
sea. He had brought along another paddle, and this I
used though my hands were so sore I could scarcely
hold it.

There was a half-moon shining, the currents were
good and the wind was at our backs. By midnight we
were nearing Pichilinque Bay and the lights of La
Paz shown faint on the horizon. It was then that the
old man suddenly looked over his shoulder. He had
done this several times since we had left the lagoon.

He lifted his arm and pointed. In a quiet voice he
said, "El Diablo."

Far astern I looked and saw the ghostly gleam of
wing-like fins.

"A manta," I said, "but not El Diablo. It is one that
I have seen around before. Last week . . ."

"It is El Diablo," the old man broke in.

He lifted his paddle and dug hard at the water and
the canoe changed direction.

"We go into Pichilinque," he said.

"But La Paz is not far," I said.

"Too far," the old man answered. "We would never reach La Paz."

Furiously he paddled and the canoe leaped forward. There was nothing I could say that would lessen the terror that had seized him. To him El Diablo was real and he was pursuing us to get back the pearl I had stolen. So I fell into the swing of his paddle and thought about the great Pearl of Heaven that I carried inside my shirt. I thought about the Sevillano and how his eyes would start out of his head when he saw it. And I wondered what my father would say and all the people of our town.

We were going through the entrance of Pichilinque. The old man said, "Do you see El Diablo?"

"No. I have looked and do not see him anywhere."

At that moment a thunderous sound engulfed the canoe. It was as if the sky had fallen in upon us. Then mounds of water rose on both sides of us and met over our heads and filled the air with spray. There followed a groan, a rending of timbers, and the canoe rose crazily and tipped and I was pitching slowly sidewise into the sea. As I fell my mind raced back to childhood. I heard my mother say, "The Manta Diablo is larger than the largest ship in the harbor. He has seven rows of teeth."

I could not see the old man but from a distance I heard him shout. My first thought was the pearl. I thrust a hand inside my shirt, fumbled around and at last found it, and set out for the shore. The old man was there ahead of me. I crawled out of the water and got to my feet and held up the pearl to show him that it was safe.

"Throw it back," he cried. "El Diablo is waiting for the pearl and he will not rest until he gets it. He is there now."

The bay was quiet. I saw nothing except the splintered canoe drifting away in the moonlight. There was no sign of the manta, and yet I knew it was one of these sea creatures that had wrecked our canoe, by chance or otherwise, for they abound in the Vermilion Sea.

"We have the pearl," I said, "and we are alive, if very wet, and if we go now we can reach La Paz by daylight."

"I do not go there with the pearl," the old man said. "I stay until morning to find the canoe. And the pearl belongs to you. I did not find it and it is not mine."

He drew back from me as if I held a serpent in my hand.

"You will change your mind," I said. "The pearl has great value."

"Never will I change my mind," he answered.

"There are three pearls lying in the shell on the beach," I said. "I forgot them."

"Those I will throw into the sea," he said.

"As you please," I said.

"And the big one you should throw there also," the old man said. "If you do not, señor, someday the Manta Diablo will have it back and your life with it. Of this I warn you."

We said farewell to each other and I started down the shore toward the lights of the town, holding the pearl tight in my hand. A rough trail led to La Paz and three leagues long, but I was there before daybreak.

I went first to the office of Salazar and Son and bolted the door behind me. I unwrapped the pearl and placed it on a piece of velvet and laid it in the scales. The pearl weighed 62.3 carats.

Then I left the office and walked up the Malecón,
the pearl hidden in my shirt. Dawn was breaking
over the mountains, but there were people on the
streets, so I greeted them as I usually do and even
stopped to talk to the woman who sells hot chocolate
outside the calabozo.

Our house is on the plaza and has a big iron gate,
which is locked at night from the inside. I rang the
bell and when one of the Indians opened it I said good
morning and strolled to the kitchen and ate a large
bowl of mush, as if nothing had happened, as if the
most beautiful pearl ever found in the Vermilion Sea
was not tucked away in my shirt.

I went to my room and put the pearl under my pillow and lay down to sleep. I tried to be calm. I tried
not to think of the pearl nor of what my father would
say nor of the Sevillano. But half the morning passed
without sleep and as I lay there I remembered suddenly that I had forgotten to lock the door of the office, so I got up and put the pearl back in my shirt
and started down the hill.

As I passed the calabozo the woman who was selling chocolate beckoned me over. Sometimes she had
small pearls to sell. She also had a long nose with
which to scent things out.

"You walk back and forth much this morning," she
said.

"It is a nice morning to walk," I answered.

She beckoned me closer. "Do you know Cantú the
fisherman who lives at Pichilinque?"

I nodded.

"Well, this Cantú, a crazy man, came by just now
and said that a great pearl has been found. Have you
heard this news?"

"Every week a great pearl is found," I said, "and every week the story is untrue."

I did not want her or anyone else to learn about the pearl until my father came back. It was he who must decide how and when the news would be given to the town. It was not proper for me as his son to take this honor from him, so I bowed respectfully and quickly left.

As I rounded the corner and started down the Malecón, I saw that a crowd was gathering outside the office of Salazar and Son. I decided to turn around and go home, but someone shouted, "Hola, Ramón."

Everyone turned to look and I knew that if I went home they would follow me, so I walked on and made my way into the crowd.

A dozen voices cried, "The Pearl. The Pearl." A dozen more cried, "Show us."

I tried to look surprised. "What pearl?" I asked.

I threw up my hands and looked puzzled and went into the office, bolted the door and put the pearl in the safe and sat down at the desk. In a moment a boy peered through the slit in the wall. He was standing on someone's shoulders and soon he began to tell the crowd what he saw. I opened the ledger and this he reported. I wrote something down and this too he reported.

Outside, the throng grew until by noon it filled the street. The boy peering in at the slit got tired and disappeared. But I sat at my desk and wrote down things that I made up, and thought of the great pearl and hoped that the fleet would come before it was time for me to leave and face the throng again.

The fleet sailed in at two o'clock. My father must have wondered about the crowd, for he was the first

ashore. He came running up the beach and as I
opened the door he burst into the office out of breath,
fearful of bad news.

"What passes?" he said.

The boy was again looking through the slit, but I
opened the safe and removed the pearl and held it
out to my father.

"This," I said.

My father took it in his hand. He turned the pearl
over in his palm and said nothing, as if he could not
believe what he saw.

"This is not a pearl," he said.

"Yes," I said, "a pearl!"

My father stared at me. "It is a joke," he said.
"There is nothing in all the seas of the world like
this." He looked at the pearl. "You have made it. You
have taken blister pearls and glued them together and
polished them carefully on a wheel. You are a very
clever young man, Ramón."

"I have glued nothing," I said. "It is a pearl. I
found it."

The boy who peered at us through the slit shouted
to the crowd, repeating my words. A shout went up
in the street. My father turned the pearl in his hand
and held it to the light and then slowly turned it
again. Then he opened the door and held up the
pearl so that the sun shone on it and all could see.

Silence fell over the crowd. There was not a sound
except the small waves breaking on the beach. Then
my father closed the door and looked at me and said,
"Madre de Dios." He said these words three times
over and sat down and stared at the great black pearl
that filled his hand.

8

When my father and I went home that evening it was like a parade. News of the monstrous pearl, found by Ramón the son of Blas Salazar, had spread through the town. It was as if the news had been written across the sky in letters of fire.

Farmers from the hills, idlers, fishermen, pearlers, merchants from their shops, women and children from everywhere, even Father Gallardo from the church, but not the Sevillano, were in the parade that followed us along the Malecón and up the hill to the plaza. Some carried torches and all sang and shouted to celebrate the great black pearl. For the town of La Paz lives by the finding and selling of pearls and therefore everyone in the town and the country around shares somehow in the fortunes of the sea.

The crowd followed us to the gates of our house and when we went in, it milled around the plaza and grew larger as more people heard the news of the pearl. It was a bigger celebration than the town has on the Cinco de Mayo.

In our home is a small workshop where my father changes gems that are not perfect and here he took the great pearl. He closed the door, so the Indian servants could not see what he was about.

First he placed the pearl on the scales and balanced the weights. "It is 62.3 in carats as you have told me," he said. "And it is exactly round. But you are wrong about its perfection." He held the pearl to the light. "Look, and you will see the smallest of flaws. It lies in the first layer or somewhere beneath, I cannot tell for certain."

I had seen the flaw already, and because I did not want to see it I had decided that it was too small to be important. "If you cut the pearl, you may find that the flaw goes deep," I said.

"If the flaw does go deep," my father said, "then it is not a great pearl. Which would you rather have, the Paragon of Pearls or just one that is good?"

"The Paragon," I said.

Still I did not wish him to cut the pearl, for I had seen many fine pearls destroyed by this cutting.

"If the flaw lies deep we have nothing," I said. "Now the flaw is small and whoever buys the pearl may never see it."

"The flaw will be seen first," my father replied, "and even though the pearl weighs more than sixty carats and is round and of rare orient and color, it is only the flaw that will be talked about. So fetch another lamp and turn up the wick on this one, and while you do this pray that God guides my hand with the knife."

I turned up the wick and lighted another lamp, as I was told to do, but I did it with my heart beating loud. From the plaza came the sound of singing and through the window I could see the flare of torches. In a moment or two, I feared, there could be nothing to celebrate, for the townspeople or for me or for anyone.

I began to pray, but somehow the words would not come. I kept hearing the old man's words, "The

Manta Diablo will have it someday, the Manta Diablo will have it back." I stared at the pearl and the knife lying beside it. Would Soto Luzon's words come true? Would the knife my father was about to use destroy the pearl forever?

My father picked up the small, sharp knife whose edge was slightly curved. He took the pearl firmly in one hand and breathed deeply and held his breath and laid the edge of the knife against the pearl. There was the faintest whisper as the knife nicked the surface. Then a peeling that was thinner than the thinnest paper came free and slowly, slowly grew in length and at last, after what seemed an hour, fell lightly upon the table.

Outside, the singing had grown louder, but here in the room there was not a sound, except the sound of my father breathing again. He put down the knife and held the pearl under the lamp and stared at it for a long time. I watched his face for some sign that the flaw had disappeared. His face did not change.

My throat was dry and choked with fear. "What do you see?" I tried to say.

He did not answer me for my words came out in a hoarse jumble that no one could understand. At last he shook his head and again picked up the knife. I walked to the window. I looked out at the night sky and began to pray.

"Watch," he said. "Someday you may need to do this yourself."

I came back to the table and stood over him and watched, still praying for the life of the great black pearl, as the knife made its slow, endless circle. Then a curled wafer fell to the table and lay there, dull in the glow of the lamp.

My father held the pearl to the light and turned it

around and around, and studied it from every angle. Suddenly he thrust the pearl high above his head, as if he wished to show it to all the world.

Then he gave the pearl to me and said, "The flaw is gone. You have in your hand the Pearl of the Universe. The Paragon of Pearls. The great Pearl of Heaven!"

9

There are four pearl dealers in our town of La Paz, as I have said, not counting Salazar and Son. There are many others of course who sell a few small pearls on the street, like the woman at the calabozo. But these are the four who buy and sell the fine pearls that come from the Vermilion Sea.

About a week after my father had cut the pearl, the four men came to our home. At first my father had talked about taking the great pearl to Mexico City, but he had done this once before with a rare pearl and the long trip had been a failure because the dealers there are very smart. So we decided to sell the Pearl of Heaven to the dealer in La Paz. Not any one of them could afford the price, nor two nor three, but the four together could raise the money we would ask.

They came early in the afternoon, dressed in their best black suits and carrying a scale and calipers and their money in a crocodile bag. The excitement in the town had died after a couple of days, but when word got around that the dealers were going to the Salazars to buy the great black pearl a crowd followed them and stood outside our gate.

My mother and my two sisters had come back from Loreto, for they too had heard the news of the pearl, and so the fountain in the patio was turned on and the parlor was fixed up with flowers and all the furniture shone.

The four men wore serious faces and they put their calipers and scales on the parlor table and their brown crocodile bag. They sat down and folded their hands and said nothing.

Then my father said, "The bag is very small, gentlemen. I doubt that it holds enough money to buy the great Pearl of Heaven."

The four dealers did not like this. One of them, named Arturo Martín, was big and shaped like a barrel and had small white hands.

"I have heard that the pearl is the size of a grapefruit," he said. "In which case we have more money than we need. For as you know the large ones are of little value."

"They do not live long, these monsters," said Miguel Palomares, who was as fat as Martín and had a bald head that glistened. "They often die or become dull before a year passes."

"And so do many of the small ones," my father said. "Like the pink one Señor Palomares sold us last month."

Señor Palomares shrugged his shoulders.

"Before I show the Pearl of Heaven," my father said, "I will tell you the price. It is twenty thousand pesos, no more and no less."

The four men looked at each other and smiled thin smiles, as if to say that they had made up their minds already about what they would pay.

My father went out of the room and came back with the pearl wrapped in a piece of white velvet. He laid it on the table in front of the four dealers.

"Now, gentlemen." With a flourish he unwrapped

the pearl and stepped back so all of them could see it. "The Pearl of Heaven!"

The great pearl caught the light, gathered it and softened it into a moon of dark fire. None of the dealers spoke for a moment or two.

Then Señor Martín said, "It is as I feared, more like a grapefruit than a pearl."

"It's a monster all right," Señor Palomares said. "The kind that often has a brief life and is very hard to sell."

One of the dealers who had not spoken cleared his throat and said, "But still we will make an offer."

The other dealers nodded solemnly.

"Ten thousand pesos," said Martín.

Señor Palomares grasped the pearl in a small, white hand and studied it.

"I think that I see a flaw," he said after a long time. "Ten thousand is too much."

"There is no flaw," my father said. "And the price, gentlemen, remains twenty thousand pesos."

The great pearl was passed around to the other dealers and they all turned it in their hands and squinted at it. At last Señor Martín used the calipers and placed the pearl on the scales. His readings were the same as I had made, almost.

"Eleven thousand pesos," he said.

"Nine thousand more is required," my father answered. "In your lives you have never seen a pearl like this one nor will you."

"Twelve thousand," said Señor Palomares.

After that and for most of an hour the price the dealers offered went up two hundred and fifty pesos at a time until the figure reached the sum of fifteen thousand pesos. And then tempers began to rise and my mother brought in a pitcher of cold juice and a platter of buñuelos. I knew that she wanted to take the dealers' offer, for I stood where I could see her in the hall making gestures to my father. She had set her mind on a beautiful red carriage and four white horses she had seen in Loreto and was fearful of losing her wish if my father did not lower the price.

Señor Martín wiped his mouth and said, "Fifteen thousand pesos is our last offer."

"Then," said my father, "I shall take the great pearl to Mexico City and ask twice that amount and sell it without haggling to dealers who know its true worth."

Señor Palomares picked up the pearl and put it down. His small head was sunk deep in the folds of his fat neck. Suddenly his head came forth like the head of a turtle and he looked at my father who was pacing back and forth.

"If you remember," he said, "you made the long journey to the City of México once before. And what did you find there? You found that the dealers are not so generous with their money as we are here in La Paz. And you came home after the long journey with your tail between your legs."

Señor Palomares got to his feet and the others followed him.

"Fifteen thousand, two hundred and fifty pesos," he said. "This is our final offer."

My father had not liked what Señor Palomares had said about the journey to Mexico City, for it had long rankled him. Nor had he liked Palomares's picture of him coming home with his tail between his legs. He stopped pacing and motioned to me.

"Go to the church," he said, "and bring Father Gallardo. Whatever he is doing, see that he comes. Go quickly."

I ran out the door and into the plaza and past the

silent crowd, not knowing why I had been sent on such an errand. I found Father Gallardo taking his afternoon siesta. I awakened him after some difficulty and dragged him back to the house. When we reached the patio I heard Señor Martín say, "We offer five hundred more," and my father answer, "The price is twenty thousand pesos."

Everybody fell silent as we came in. The four dealers, who had their heads together, looked up. Señor Palomares was holding the pearl and my father strode over and took it from him. Then my father turned to the priest and bowed.

"Here is the Pearl of Heaven," he said. "My son and I give it to you so that you may give it to the Madonna, our beloved Lady-of-the-Sea, to hold and keep forever."

A scream went up from the hallway. I think it was my mother who screamed, but it might have been my sister, for she too had been dreaming of things she wished to buy. Then the four men silently picked up their instruments and the brown crocodile bag filled with money and put on their hats and left. As he took the great pearl, Father Gallardo tripped over his long robe and began to stutter. As for me, I had not wished for anything especially, so I looked at my father and felt proud that he had bested the four dealers.

Then Father Gallardo recovered his voice and tried to speak calmly.

"We will celebrate the pearl," he said. "It will be the most wondrous celebration La Paz has ever seen in all its history."

But my mother was not pleased with the gift of the pearl nor was she pleased with the idea of celebrating the gift. She ran into the parlor after Father Gallardo had left and tears were in her eyes.

"The beautiful pearl is gone," she sobbed.

"Not gone," said my father. "It will be in the church for everyone to see. And you can go there and see it too."

"I do not wish to see it again," my mother cried. "The Madonna has many pearls. You could have given Her a smaller one."

"Because She has only small pearls, I gave Her a big pearl," my father said.

My mother went over to where he stood and looked up at him and wiped the tears from her eyes.

"That is not the reason," she said. "You gave the great pearl because you were angry with the dealers. You gave it away to spite them."

"No, it was a gift from the House of Salazar," my father said proudly. "And for this gift of the great pearl, the greatest pearl ever found in all the Vermilion Sea, the House of Salazar shall be favored in Heaven, now and forever."

My mother said nothing more, but when Father Gallardo held his celebration she felt a headache and stayed at home.

10

Father Gallardo's celebration took place five days later.

The church blazed with candles, and flowers decked the altar, and the air was sweet with incense. The young Madonna stood in Her niche dressed in a white satin gown, with garlands of daisies braided through Her hair. In Her outstretched hand lay the great black pearl.

The church was filled and the people flowed through the big door and out into the plaza. Never before had our town of La Paz seen such a multitude. They came on foot, on burro and on horseback from as far away as Loreto in the north and Santo Tomás in the south. They even came by canoe from the bare islands of the Vermilion Sea. And there were also a band of Indians from the wild barrancas of the Sierra Morena dressed in rabbit skins. Their presence pleased Father Gallardo.

"The pearl has worked a miracle," he said. "For many years I have tried to coax these savages into my church but failed."

After the services the Madonna was placed on a bower festooned with flowers and borne twice around the plaza while the people sang and danced. Then

She was carried down to the sea to bless the Salazar fleet.

This was my father's idea, the blessing of the fleet. It was to show my mother that the great black pearl already had won the favor of Heaven, and a sign that the House of Salazar would always prosper.

And this is why the Madonna was borne down to the sea, and on the shore Father Gallardo stood beside the Madonna with the crowd gathered around him. On the quiet water of the bay rode our five blue boats, each one fresh-painted and strung with streamers of bright paper.

"We ask Your protection for these boats," Father Gallardo said, raising his arms. "Speed them to the pearling grounds and bring them safely home. We ask that You bless the House of Salazar that has so honored our church this day, that they may find another pearl as large as the one they have given."

After Father Gallardo had blessed the fleet, the Madonna was carried through the streets again. In Her hand lay the Pearl of Heaven so that everyone could see it once more. And to the throng that gathered around the Madonna and Her pearl, as the procession wound back to the church, it was a wonderful day. For to those who had little and to those who had nothing, the pearl also belonged to each of them, to dream of the rest of their lives.

When the Madonna was placed in Her niche, I knelt before Her and gave thanks that I had found the pearl that so many now would cherish for their own. And as I walked out of the church, if for a moment I imagined all the boats the pearl would have bought, enough to build a dozen fleets, it was a thought that quickly vanished.

The Sevillano called to me. He was standing outside the church, dressed in tight trousers and a ruffled shirt that was open and showed the tattoos on his chest.

"Well, mate," he said, "it has been a big day, almost as big as the day I found the pearl in the Gulf of Persia. I have heard many stories about your pearl, but how much does it really weigh?"

I told him the true weight, though I felt that whatever I said the one he had found would be larger.

"The pearl from the gulf," he said, "was heavier. Picture one that filled your two hands, and that was the pearl I sold to the Shah of Persia."

"A good one," I said, and as I spoke I was surprised that I did not feel the same about the Sevillano. His bragging no longer annoyed me, or not nearly so much. And now that I had dived in the Vermilion Sea and found the great black pearl, he could not say that I had done nothing nor that I was a coward. "What did it weigh?" I asked him.

"I have forgotten," he said, looking at his boots, suddenly not interested in weights. "Tell me, does your pearl have a flaw?"

"It is not my pearl."

The Sevillano was a scoffer, and this was his way of saying that he did not believe in the Madonna.

"Sure, I know all about that. But does it have a flaw?"

"None," I said.

"Not the smallest?"

"None."

"Is it truly round?"

"Yes."

"A round pearl that has no flaws and weighs more

than sixty carats is worth . . ." He whispered through
his teeth. Then he lowered his voice. "I have heard
you found it at Pichilinque."

"Nearby," I said.

And though he pressed me I would say no more, so
we parted with a handshake and I started home.
Night was falling. As I drew near the gate a figure
stepped out of the shadows and spoke my name. It
was the old man from the lagoon, Soto Luzon.

"Did you like the celebration?" I asked him.

He did not speak at once and then not to answer
me.

"I saw the Madonna and the pearl," he said. "I saw
them go through the plaza and through the streets
and down to the sea and I heard everyone singing."
He reached out and put a hand on my shoulder. "You
are still a boy and there is much that you do not
know. Therefore I must tell you that the pearl does
not belong to the Madonna nor to the church nor to
the people who were singing. It belongs to the Manta
Diablo and someday he will take it back. Of this I
solemnly warn you."

I began to say something, but without another
word the old man turned and disappeared into the
darkness. I thought no more about him until morning
when my father and I were walking down to the
beach.

"Would Luzon allow me to search for pearls in the
lagoon?" my father said.

"No, and I would not ask him."

"The voyage to Cerralvo is long," my father said.
"Our last trip there gave us few pearls, though more
than elsewhere. In the lagoon we might find another
like the great one."

I told my father about the encounter with the old man the night before and what he had said.

"Luzon is a crazy Indian," my father replied.

"Crazy or not," I said, "it is his lagoon and he will not allow you to dive there."

11

The fleet sailed that morning for Isla Cerralvo. The boats glistened in their fresh paint and the streamers that hung from their masts still shone bright. They fluttered in a light wind that blew out of the south, and the sky was the same color as the morning sea. It was a beautiful day, as if the Madonna Herself had willed it so.

When I left for home that afternoon it was very hot, because the south wind had died away. Then the cool coromuel started to blow down from the mountains. But at supper the coromuel died too and the air was heavy and hard to breathe. Trailing clouds appeared in the sky and the palms in the courtyard began to rustle.

My mother stopped eating and went to the window and looked out. If my father was on the sea the smallest change in the weather made her fearful. If the wind did blow she was fearful. If the wind did not blow or the sky was overcast with mackerel clouds or morning dawned without haze, she was fearful.

"It is the coromuel again," I said.

"The coromuel is cool," she answered. "The wind in the palms is hot."

"It is hot because the night is hot," I said, though I knew better. I knew that it was in this way that the chubasco began, the most dreaded wind that blows on our Vermilion Sea. "I will go outside and look, but I am sure that it is the coromuel."

In the courtyard, I glanced at the sky. There were no stars and the wind had died once more. Yet I was aware that the wind that had rustled the palms was not a mountain wind. It had come from the south-west, home of the chubasco, for the air smelled strong of the sea.

I went back to my supper and tried hard to be cheerful. "The sky is clear," I said. "I have never seen so many stars. It is a fine night on the sea."

"The palms rustle again," my mother said.

The gentle sound filled the room for a time as we drank our chocolate. Then, as if the palm leaves had turned to iron, there came a sound of metal clashing against metal.

I got up and started across the room to close the door, but before I had taken two steps the door crashed shut. The candle flames moved back and forth and then were snuffed out by an unseen hand. I tried to relight the candles but failed, for through the barred window the air was being sucked from the room in great sighs.

"The wind," my mother said.

"The chubasco," my sister whispered.

I went to the window and looked out. There were no stars and the clashing of the palms could not be heard. The sound was lost in the voice of the wind that had become the screams of a thousand frightened gulls.

"The fleet had warning," I said. "It has put in at Pichilinque or one of the safe coves. There are many between here and Cerralvo."

My mother got up and tried to open the door.

"Help me," she cried.

"You could not go farther than the courtyard," I told her. "Not that far, even crawling on your hands and knees. The fleet is safe, never fear. It has the best captain on the sea and he has been through many chubascos."

The screaming of the wind became so loud that we could not hear each other. We huddled around the table in the dark room and did not try to talk. The Indians came from the kitchen and sat on the floor beside us. Two of them had husbands with the fleet.

At midnight the wind still raged, but toward morning it slackened and at dawn died away in gasps, as a wounded beast dies. We all started for the harbor, to be there when the fleet came home. In the courtyard the palms were stripped of their leaves, and tiles from the roof lay scattered around, and when we reached the plaza pieces of rooftops were lying there also.

The morning was gray and hot. As we hurried down to the beach, many people joined us. Some of them had husbands or brothers with the fleet and all had friends. The beach was strewn with sea kelp and rows of dead fish and the boats that had been anchored in the harbor were piled high on the shore. Usually, before a chubasco the boats were pulled out of the water and tied down with rocks. But the storm had struck so fast that this could not be done.

Father Gallardo came running down to the beach shortly after we got there. His white hair stood on end and he had his robe kilted up to his knees, yet he spoke to us hopefully, telling us that the boats would soon be sailing in.

"The Madonna has watched over the fleet," he said, "and it is safe. There are no coves here at hand, so it will be afternoon before the boats can reach the harbor. Go now to your homes with hope, and with faith in our Madonna, and wait."

But no one left the beach. The morning passed and the afternoon wore on and then at sunset someone sighted a boat far out beyond the lizard's tongue. The boat came closer and rounded the lizard's tongue and I saw that it was Soto Luzon in his red canoe.

The old man pulled his canoe up the shore, far from the people who were gathered there, and sat down. I went over to him and asked him if he had seen anything of the fleet.

He rolled a cornhusk cigarette and puffed on it for a time. "I have not seen the fleet," he said. "Nor will I ever see it again, nor will you, señor."

Anger came over me at these words. "Do you say that the manta wrecked the fleet?"

"No, señor, I do not say this. The storm wrecked the fleet and you will never see it again."

"But you mean that the manta called up the storm."

The old man did not answer. In anger I walked away and left him and went back to where the people were gathered. At nightfall he was still there on the sand, smoking his cigarettes and waiting.

We built a fire out of driftwood and all of us stood around it. The crowd grew larger and some friends brought food and water down to us from the town. And Father Gallardo came with a cross, which he placed upright in the sand as a symbol of our hope.

My mother said to him, "My husband gave the great pearl to the Madonna. Surely, father, She will bring him home."

"Yes, surely," he said. "For this was a wonderful gift."

The night wore on and many from the town drifted away. We kept the fire bright until dawn, hoping that it would help the fleet to find the harbor safely. Dawn broke clear and the sea lay quiet between the head-lands and the peaks of the far-off islands seemed to float in the sky, so close that you could reach out a hand and touch them.

Soon after sunrise a boy standing on the seawall pointed to the south. I looked and saw a lone figure stumbling along the shore. At first I thought it was some drunken sailor who had strayed in from the town. He was shirtless and his face was covered with blood and he would fall, lie for a moment, and get up. But as he came closer there was something about him I remembered.

I ran down the shore. It was Gaspar Ruiz, the Sevillano, and as I reached him he fell at my feet. He raised himself and looked up at me. I have never seen the eyes of a living man that held in them so much terror.

He opened his mouth and closed it and then he said, "Lost. The fleet is lost," and fell back on the sand and began to mutter words that I could not hear.

12

Among the thirty-two men of the Salazar fleet, driven on the rocks of Punta Maldonado, only one survived, the Sevillano.

On the fourth day after the storm, services were held for our dead. The church again was decorated with flowers and filled with people from the town and the hills, and many who could not find a place stood outside. How strange, everyone said, that in less than a month the two greatest happenings in all the history of La Paz had taken place. First it was the finding of the great pearl. Then it was the coming of the great storm that wrecked the fleet and drowned so many. Nobody could put what he thought into words, but there were those who felt that the two happenings were joined together in some mysterious way.

Of these, I was one. And as I knelt beside my mother while Father Gallardo spoke on that sad morning, I listened with only half my heart to what he said.

My eyes were fixed upon the Madonna. She stood in Her niche all dressed in white and on Her face was a smile, the sweet smile that I often had seen before. She looked out at the kneeling mourners, smiling as if nothing ever had happened to the fleet and its men on the rocks of Punta Maldonado.

Father Gallardo was speaking of my father and his generous gifts to the church, especially the gift of the beautiful pearl. At that moment a ray of light fell through a window full upon the Madonna. It shone upon the pearl She held in Her hand and set it aglow, and as I gazed at the pearl I began to wonder for the first time why such a magnificent gift had not protected my father against the storm.

I wondered about this as I filed out of the church with the others, and as I stood in the plaza and talked to some of my friends, and when the Sevillano came up to me and put his hand on my shoulder, I was still wondering why the Madonna and Her pearl had failed to stay the coming of the storm.

"The big Pearl of Heaven," the Sevillano said, "did not bring us luck."

Always before I had paid no heed to his scoffing, but now his words somehow echoed what I was thinking. And yet I drew myself up and spoke to him sharply.

"The Pearl brought *you* luck," I said. "Or else you would not be here among the living."

"It was not the pearl," he said. "I am here because I am a good swimmer."

While we stood there, now saying little to each other, I saw at a distance the old man walking quietly up and down. He kept casting a glance over the departing throng and toward the church, but never at me, as if he did not know that I was there. And yet when I left the Sevillano I heard steps and turned to see him not three feet away.

"I tell you this once more," the old man said, "the pearl belongs to the Manta Diablo. And I tell *you* because it is *you* who found the pearl."

I made no reply to him and soon lost myself in the

crowd. I did not go home as I had planned to do to be with my mother and sister, but went back to the church instead. I thought I would talk to Father Gallardo and tell him of the doubts that had overtaken me. He was not in his cell behind the altar, nor could I find him anywhere.

As I came to the niche where the Madonna stood I knelt and closed my eyes, but all I could think of was the boats lying broken on the rocks of Maldonado and my father dead and the old man's warning. I opened my eyes and looked up at the Madonna. I looked at the pearl She held in her hand, outstretched as if She wished me or someone to take it.

I rose and glanced around the church. It was deserted. I called Father Gallardo's name, but got no answer. Then quickly I reached out, grasped the pearl, lifted it from the Madonna's hand, thrust it deep inside my pocket, and walked softly down the aisle.

I had closed the big door when I came in and now as I opened it and took two steps, I found myself face to face with the Sevillano.

"I go back to get my sombrero," he said, "if someone in this town of thieves has not already stolen it."

I stepped aside for him to pass. He drew back and looked at me. It was only a fleeting look, but as I walked on I asked myself if in that quick glance he had not seen the bulge the pearl made in my pocket.

I crossed the plaza, turning around several times, for I half-expected the old man to be following me, and as I reached the gate I looked for him to step out from the trees.

The great pearl was found missing early that evening by an altar boy. I knew that someone had dis-

covered the theft for the big bell in the church began
to toll.

At the first sound of the bell my mother who was
writing a letter dropped her pen and looked at me.

"What does the bell mean?" she asked.

"It calls the town to prayer."

"This is not the hour for prayer."

"Then some boys are playing around in the belfry,"
I said.

The bell went on tolling and in a short time Father
Gallardo came to the door, out of breath.

"The pearl is gone," he cried. "Gone!"

"Gone?" I asked.

"Stolen!"

I jumped to my feet and followed him back to the
church. People were gathering outside. He led me
down the aisle and pointed to the niche where the
Madonna stood with Her hand held out and empty. A
crowd had followed us and there were many ideas
about who had stolen the great pearl. Someone said
that an Indian she knew had stolen it. Another said
he had seen a strange man running away from the
church.

As I listened and the women wept and Father Gallardo wrung his hands, it was on my tongue to say, "I
have the pearl. It is in my room, hidden under my
pillow. Wait and I will get it." Then I thought of the
wrecked ships at Maldonado and again I heard the
old man's voice, as clear as if he were there in the
church beside me, speaking his solemn admonition.

I slipped away and went home and after supper,
with the pearl hidden in my shirt, I went down to the
beach, taking a roundabout path so as not to be seen.
I searched until I found a boat that belonged to a man
I knew. It was not a boat for a swift voyage, being

too large for me to handle well, but there were no others.

When the moon came up I started for the lagoon where the Manta Diablo lived, or where the old man said he lived, and now I half-believed to be the truth.

13

About dawn I reached the entrance to the lagoon. The tide was out but it had started to change and I had trouble steering the boat down the dark channel.

As I came to the rocks that guard the cave, I found that the lagoon lay hidden under a mantle of red mist, so heavy that the far shore where the old man lived could not be seen. It was then that I heard a sound. Perhaps I heard nothing and only felt that someone or something was behind me.

During the long night I had thought little of the Manta Diablo and when I did it was without fear. A creature who could change his form and become a living person and go into the town and even into the church, as the old man said, whose friends among the sharks and fish told him everything they saw or heard on the sea, surely this creature would know that I had the great pearl and was returning it to his cave. Still from time to time, as I rowed southward in the night, I scanned the moonlit waves for the monstrous, bat-like form, half-smiling as I did so.

Behind me in the mist I heard the sound again. Then above the hissing of the tide came a voice I knew at once.

"Good morning, mate," he said. "But you are slow with the oars. I followed you out from La Paz and dawdled most of the night and waited and fell asleep. Does the pearl weigh you down?"

"What pearl?" I asked, calmly as I could.

The Sevillano laughed. "The great one, of course," he said. "Listen and let us be truthful. I know that you stole the big one. I stood at the door and saw you steal it and I also saw the bulge in your pocket when you came out from the church. Since we are truthful and you will wonder why I watched you I must say that I was there because I came to steal the pearl myself. Does that surprise you?"

"No," I said.

"Two thieves," the Sevillano said and laughed again. "Now that we both speak the truth as thieves, do you have the pearl?"

I could not see him through the heavy mist nor could I judge where his boat was.

"And if you do not have the pearl," he said, "then tell me, is this where you found it?" His voice became hard. "To both these questions, give me a truthful answer."

Now the red mist parted a little where we were floating and the sun broke through. The Sevillano was between me and the manta's cave, much closer than I had thought him to be. In his hand was a knife and the sun glittered on it. We looked at each other and I saw by his face that he meant to use the knife if the need arose; still I said nothing.

"Do not think that I blame you for stealing the great pearl," he said. "For all the good it did it might better have been given to the devil. Nor do I blame you for wishing to keep the place where you found it a secret. But hand it over, mate, and we shall talk then about other things."

He put the knife in his belt. His boat moved nearer,

until it touched the prow of mine. He held out his hand to take the pearl.

The cave was dark, yet not far distant, so I could see it clearly. I took the pearl from my shirt, as if to give it to him, but as he put out his hand to receive it, I threw the pearl into the air, beyond him into the water, into the mouth of the cave.

It was an unwise thing to do, for the pearl had no quicker left my hand than the Sevillano was in the sea, swimming beneath the water. I picked up the oars and turned the heavy boat against the current, thinking that I would row to the far end of the lagoon and seek the old man's help. Before I could straighten the boat, the Sevillano came to the surface, grasped one of the oars and then the gunwale. In his hand was the great black pearl.

"You toss it to the devil and the devil picks it up," he said, climbing over the side. "Now we find my boat."

It had drifted off on the tide. The boat was smaller than mine and as we overtook it I saw that it was filled with provisions for a voyage—food, a jug of water, a fishing line and hooks, and an iron harpoon, among other things. The Sevillano stepped into the boat and motioned me to follow. Not knowing what he meant for me, I did not move.

"Hurry, mate, or we miss the tide," he said. "We have many leagues to go."

"I am rowing ashore," I answered him. "I have business with Soto Luzon."

The Sevillano slipped a knife from his belt. I looked toward the far shore and hoped that the old man had heard our talk and had come to the lagoon to see who we were, but the red mist still hid the shore from view.

Again the Sevillano motioned me into the boat, this time with his threatening knife. I had no choice except to obey him.

"Sit down. Be comfortable," he said, handing me a pair of oars.

He stripped off his singlet and wrapped it round the pearl and seated himself in back of me.

"Row," he said.

The mist had begun to rise from the water. I took a last look toward the shore, but it was deserted. Then I felt the sharp point of the knife pressing against my shoulder. I picked up the oars and began to row aimlessly.

"Toward the sea," the Sevillano said. "Because we go in that direction. And why do we go in that direction? Since you will ask this sooner or later, I shall tell you now. We go to the City of Guaymas. What do we there? We sell the great pearl. We sell it together, you and I, for the name of Salazar is known among the pearl dealers of Guaymas. And for this reason we shall sell it for ten times the sum I could get if I sold it alone."

He was silent, busying himself with his oars. I heard him set the oars in their locks and thought, Now there is a chance for me to slip over the side and swim to the nearest shore. He must have read my thoughts, for again I felt the knife pressing against my back.

"Since I cannot row and watch at the same time," he said, "it is you who must do the rowing, so put your mind to it, mate. The tide turns and does not wait."

Slowly I pulled at the oars, thinking a hundred thoughts in desperation. But to no avail, for the knife was at my back and I could only do what I was bidden.

Once outside the channel, too far for me to swim ashore, the Sevillano set his course eastward across the Vermilion and raised a ragged sail.

14

The wind blew fresh from the south and we made a goodly distance that morning. At noon we ate some of the corn cakes the Sevillano had brought and then I lay down and slept. When I awoke at dusk I asked the Sevillano if he wished me to take the tiller while he slept.

"No," he said and grinned. "I have little trust in you, mate. I might never wake up and if I did I would most likely find that you had turned the boat around and we were sailing back into La Paz."

Nevertheless, the Sevillano did doze off, but with one eye open and a hand on his knife and the pearl held between his bare feet, which had long toes like fingers.

The wind slackened and as the moon came up I saw a movement on the sea, some two furlongs astern. It was not a wave that I saw because the sea was smooth. There were many sharks around, so I thought that a few of them were feeding upon a school of fish. Shortly I saw the movement again and this time the moon's light shone on the tips of outspread wing-like fins, rising and slowly falling. It was plainly a manta.

We had seen several of these creatures that day, sunning themselves or leaping high into the air out of good spirits, therefore I paid no heed to the one swimming behind us. I fell asleep and awoke about midnight to sounds that I felt I had dreamed.

The sounds were small and not far distant, like the sounds that wavelets make as they slide upon a beach. Suddenly I found that they were nothing I had dreamed, for not more than a hundred feet away and clear in the moonlight a giant manta was swimming along behind us.

"We have a companion," I said.

"A big one," replied the Sevillano. "I wish he would swim out in front and then I could tie a rope to him and we would soon be in the City of Guaymas."

He laughed at the picture he had called up, but I sat silent and stared at the giant manta swimming close to the stern of our boat. That it was the same manta I had seen early in the evening, I had no doubt.

"He smells the corn cakes," said the Sevillano.

At daylight the manta still swam behind us. He was no closer than before, swimming along at the same pace as the boat, with only the slightest movement of his fins, more like a giant bat swimming through the air than like a fish.

"Remember on the voyage," I said to the Sevillano, "when we were coming home and you shouted, 'Manta Diablo,' and the Indian got scared? Well, he should be here now to se. this one."

"I have seen many," said the Sevillano, "but this one is the monster of all. He will measure ten paces across, from fin to fin, and weigh more than two ton. But they are a chummy sort, these sea-bats, friendly like the dolphins. I have had them follow my boat for a whole day, yet never with malice. Still, with a mere flip of a fin or a twitch of their tail they can send you into eternity."

Most of an hour went by and then the manta swam out ahead of us. As he passed the boat, I clearly saw his eyes. They were the color of amber and flecked with black spots and they seemed to fix themselves upon me and me alone, not upon the Sevillano. I also caught a glimpse of his mouth and for some reason remembered that my mother had told me that the Manta Diablo had seven rows of teeth, and I said to myself, "She was wrong, he has no teeth above and only one set below, which is dull and not sharp like knives and very white."

The manta turned and came back, swimming in a wide circle around us. Then out he went again, but this time when he returned the circle was smaller and the waves he made caused the boat to pitch about.

"I grow tired of our friend," said the Sevillano. "If he swims closer I will give him a taste of the harpoon."

I wanted to say to the Sevillano, "You had best not molest him. One harpoon would be only the prick of a pin." I tried to say, "This is not just a manta that swims there. This is the Manta Diablo." But my lips were frozen.

I think it was the amber eye he had fixed upon me as he passed, upon me and not upon the Sevillano. Yet it might have been the stories that had frightened me as a child, before I had learned to laugh at them, that now came flooding back, more real than they ever were. I do not know. I do know that suddenly I was certain that the giant swimming there was the Manta Diablo himself.

The circles grew smaller. We were the center of them—the boat, the Sevillano, myself, the pearl—of this I had no doubt.

The boat began to rock violently and water came in

and we both had to bail with our hats to save it from sinking. A half mile or less off our bow was an island called Isla de los Muertos, Island of the Dead. It had gained this name because on it lived a tribe of Indians who were known to do away with all those who landed there, to spear turtles or for any other reason.

"Keep at the bailing and I will row," said the Sevillano. "We head for the island."

"I would rather take my chances on Los Muertos," I said and never in my life meant anything more.

As if he sensed what we planned to do, the Manta Diablo swam off to a distance, sank out of sight, and allowed us to reach the island safely.

15

Los Muertos is barren like all the islands of our Vermilion Sea, but it has a snug, sandy cove where turtles by the hundreds come to lay their eggs. Into this we made our way, beached the boat, and then climbed a low hill behind the cove, which gives a good view of the island.

Isla de los Muertos is small and mostly flat and at its southern end the Indians live out in the open, without shelters of any kind. From the hill we saw that evening fires were burning and people had gathered around them and that their black canoes lay in a neat row on the shore. We decided, therefore, that no one had seen us sail into the cove.

We turned the boat over and emptied the water that had almost swamped us and ate more of the corn cakes. By then it was night.

"We wait for an hour," said the Sevillano. "That will give the manta time to find another boat to follow."

"We can wait for an hour or for a day," I said, "but he will be there still."

"What do you mean?"

"I mean that the one out there is the Manta Diablo."

It was too dark to see his face, but I knew that the

Sevillano was staring at me as though I had lost all my senses.

"Santa Maria!" he cried. "I am aware that ignorant Indians believe in the Manta Diablo. But that you who have been to school and can read books, one of the mighty Salazars himself, should believe this fairy tale. Santa Rosalia, it surprises me!"

"Furthermore," I said, "he is waiting out there for the pearl and he will wait until he gets it."

The Sevillano was leaning against the boat. He stood up and came over to where I sat.

"If I throw the pearl into the sea," he said, "the manta will take it, swim away and leave us alone. Is that what you are getting at?"

"Yes."

The Sevillano turned his back and walked over to the boat and gave it a thump with his foot, I guess to show his disgust. He then strolled off in the dark, as if he wished to be as far away from me as possible.

The moon rose. Soon afterwards, from the hill above, I heard the soft cries and rustle of birds. Something had disturbed the terns that had flown in at sunset to nest. As I glanced up, I saw a figure outlined against the sky.

I jumped to my feet, but did not call to the Sevillano. Here was a chance to rid myself of him. I could climb the hill and tell the Indian who stood there why I had landed on the island. He might give me help, for he would understand about the Manta Diablo.

It was a dangerous plan, yet it might have succeeded had not the Sevillano seen the Indian, too.

"We go!" he shouted.

I hesitated a moment, watching the Indian on the hill above me. The nesting terns began to scream and flutter about, so I was certain that other Indians had come up from the village to join him.

The Sevillano ran to the boat and turned it over and stowed the supplies that lay on the sand.

"Hurry," he shouted at me.

I walked over to the boat and helped him shove it into the water. Where the pearl was I did not know, whether hidden in the boat or in his pocket.

"Perhaps you would like to stay," the Sevillano said. "The Indians of Los Muertos dig a pit in the sand and put you in it up to your chin and then let the turtles nibble at your face. But maybe you would like this better than the Manta Diablo."

The boat was floating and the Sevillano had picked up the oars.

"Do you go or stay?" he said.

A shower of arrows came whistling down from the hill and struck the sand. There was nothing for me to do now except to scramble into the boat, which I did just as a second flight of arrows churned the water around us.

The moon was near to full and the air was clear and the sea stretched away like a bed of silver. There were no signs of the Manta Diablo. The Sevillano put up the sail, though the wind had died, and both of us rowed hard, fearing that the Indians would launch their canoes. For a long time we heard their shouts, but they did not try to follow us.

When we left the lee of the island, we picked up a light breeze. The Sevillano reset the sail and took a sight on the North Star and steered the boat eastward along the moon's path.

16

At sunrise the island of Los Muertos lay behind us. The air was heavy and scarcely a ripple showed on the sea. Over and around us hung a thin, red mist, but I did not locate the Manta Diablo until more than an hour had passed.

It was then that a needlefish, longer than my arm, skimmed the water and flew by me like a bullet. I heard the chattering of its green teeth and as I turned around to see what ever could have frightened a fish that is noted for its courage, the water heaved up half a furlong behind the boat. From this hillock rose the manta.

Through a shower of foam he rose high into the air, higher than I ever had seen one leap before, so high that I could see the flash of his white undersides and his long tail whipping about. There he seemed to rest for a moment or two, as if to survey all that lay about him, then down he came and struck the water a thunderous blow.

"Your friend shows off," said the Sevillano.

He spoke calmly and I looked at him, wondering that now, even now he did not know that it was the Manta Diablo who had leaped into the air and why he had done so.

The Sevillano took the pearl from between his feet

and wedged it behind the jug of water in the stern of the boat and picked up the harpoon.

"I have killed nine mantas," he said. "They are much easier to kill than whales of the same size, because they lack the blubber of the whale. They are also easier to kill than the thresher shark or the six-gill or seven-gill shark or the tiger shark or the big gray one."

The Manta Diablo sank from view. It was nearly noon before I saw him again. A light wind came up and ruffled the sea and it might have been that he swam there close behind us all the time the Sevillano was telling me how simple it was to kill a manta and where he had killed the nine.

I first saw the outstretched wings and then he passed the boat and I saw the amber eyes turn and look at me as they had once before. They said as clearly as if the words were spoken, "The pearl is mine. Throw it into the sea. It has brought you ill fortune and ill fortune will be yours until you give it back."

I must have muttered something at this moment that betrayed my fear, for the Sevillano squinted his eyes and studied me. He was certain at last that he had a child or a crazy man to deal with.

The Manta Diablo swam by just out of range of the harpoon. Majestically he swam on ahead of us and came slowly back in a wide circle. The Sevillano waited for him with his feet spread apart and one leg braced against the tiller and the heavy harpoon in his hand.

The pearl lay beyond my reach. I would need to crawl the length of the boat to get at it. Any movement I made now he would see, so I decided to wait

until the Manta Diablo drew closer and the Sevillano
would have his mind fixed upon him.

Again the Sevillano looked at me. "I am beginning
to understand a few things," he said in his soft voice,
patiently as if he were talking to a child or someone
bereft. "You stole the pearl from the Madonna because She failed to protect the fleet of your father.
You traveled all night to the lagoon where you had
found the pearl. And you went there to give it back
to the Manta Diablo. Is this right?"

I did not answer him.

"Well," he said, "let me tell you something. It is
news that you do not know, that no one knows except
Gaspar Ruiz." He was silent for a moment, watching
the Manta Diablo. "But for one small matter, at this
very hour the fleet might be sailing under these same
skies or riding safely at anchor in the harbor of La
Paz. And your father might be sitting down in his
patio to a feast of roast pig and good wine from
Jerez."

Anger seized me. I sat quietly and did not move,
but the Sevillano saw it on my face.

"Calm yourself," he said, "for I only wish to tell you
why the fleet was wrecked upon the rocks of Punta
Maldonado. A better one never sailed the Vermilion.
Your father was a fine captain. Yet ships and men and
your father all went down in a storm no worse than
others they had lived through. Why, you ask."

"I ask nothing."

"But I will tell you, mate, because it may take me
some time to get rid of the manta. While I am busy
and not keeping a watchful eye, you might get a
crazy idea. You might take the pearl and throw it
overboard. Then I would have to slit your throat.

That would be a shame, for the manta did not cause your father's death."

The Manta Diablo was still a good distance away and seemed in no hurry to overtake us, idly lifting and lowering his beautiful dark fins. But the Sevillano fastened one end of the harpoon rope and coiled the rest in a neat pile at his feet.

"When the storm was gathering," he said, "when the whole southern sky was filled with fearsome clouds, I told your father that we should turn back and seek shelter at Las Ánimas. He laughed at me. The wind, he said, was with us and we could reach port before the storm struck. It was a bad decision, he made. And he made it because of the pearl, because of his gift to the Madonna. Not that he ever spoke of the pearl. Oh, no, not once did he mention it while we stood and argued and the wind blew and the clouds banked higher. But all the time the black pearl was there in his mind. I could tell it was there, big and important. I could tell by the way he spoke."

The Sevillano paused and raised his chin, striking a pose to show how my father had looked. It reminded me of the moment in the parlor when he had given the pearl to Father Gallardo and afterwards when he told my mother that the House of Salazar would be favored in Heaven, now and forever.

"I could tell," the Sevillano went on, "by the way he spoke, so sure about the storm and everything, that he felt, he knew that God had hold of his hand."

The Sevillano ran a finger over the iron barb of the harpoon and sighted along the shaft and made a few practice thrusts in the air. While he was doing these things, he said, "If you had the choice to make over again, would you steal the pearl from the Madonna?"

I hesitated to answer him, confused as I was by

what I had just heard and by his question. Before I
could speak, he said,

"No, Ramón Salazar would not steal the pearl. Of
course not, now that he knows why the fleet was
wrecked. Nor would he steal the pearl from his good
pal, Gaspar Ruiz."

The Sevillano waited for me to answer, but I was
silent. I sat in the bow of the boat and watched the
Manta Diablo swimming effortlessly along behind us.
Already I had decided what I would do if he killed
the Manta Diablo or if he failed. Whether it was one
or the other, I now saw clearly how I must act and
that this I would not tell him.

17

The Manta Diablo swam by once more, again just out of reach, and made a wide circle and came back. As he overtook the boat for the third time that morning, he passed closer than before. It seemed that this time he was daring the Sevillano to throw the harpoon, for the amber eyes of the monster were fixed upon him and not upon me.

The Sevillano gave a loud grunt and I heard the harpoon leave his hand and the rope twisted like a snake and shot upwards. A loop caught my foot and I was thrown against the bulwarks. I thought for an instant that I would be dragged into the sea, but somehow the rope came loose.

Sprawled against the side of the boat, I saw the long harpoon curve outward and down and then sink. It struck the Manta Diablo squarely between his outspread wings.

A moment later the rope which held the harpoon snapped taut and the boat leaped from the sea and fell back with a shudder that rattled my teeth. It then slid back and forth, but once the rope tightened again, it began to move forward.

"Your friend takes us in the right direction," said the Sevillano and settled down at the tiller as if he were on his way to a fiesta. "At this rate we should be in Guaymas by tomorrow."

But the Manta Diablo swam eastward for only a short distance and then turned and headed into the west. He swam slowly, so that no water came aboard, as if he did not wish to disturb us in any way. He swam along a path straighter than I could have charted with a compass, toward the place we both knew well.

"Now your friend takes us in the wrong direction," said the Sevillano. "However, they soon grow tired, these mantas."

Nonetheless, the morning wore on and noon came and still the Manta Diablo swam slowly westward.

About this time the Sevillano became restless. He no longer lounged at the tiller, his broad-brimmed hat cocked on one side. Instead, he handed over the tiller to me and took a place in the bow which gave him a better view of the sea-beast and the harpoon it treated like the prick of a pin.

From time to time he would say something to himself and then glance at me with a curious glint in his eyes. I began to wonder if at last he knew that his adversary was not one of the common mantas, which he had little respect for, but *the* Manta, the Manta Diablo itself.

I did not have long to wonder. As we came abreast of Isla de los Muertos, he jumped to his feet and drew the long, cork-handled knife from his belt. I thought he meant to cut the rope that bound us to the untiring monster. And for an instant this may have been in his mind, but then with an oath he put the knife away and started to haul on the rope, hand over hand.

One hard-earned length at a time, he pulled the

boat forward. The Manta Diablo did not change his pace nor his course through the quiet sea, so steadily we overtook him. In the end we were so near that I could have reached up and grasped his curved, rat-like tail.

At this point, the Sevillano tied the rope securely at the bow. He tossed his hat aside and took off his shirt and took the knife from his belt. He then filled his lungs with air and let it out with a sigh, thrice over, as if he were going down for a long dive.

All this was done with a false smile and a flourish, like a magician getting ready for an act. I had the feeling he had vowed to himself that he would kill the Manta Diablo, no matter how long it took or at what cost. He would kill it to show that after all Gaspar Ruiz was more of a man than I could ever hope to be.

I thought I had forgotten our old rivalry, that when I found the great pearl the feud between us had come to an end. I was wrong, it had not ended.

Sitting there with my hands folded, as I watched him prepare to kill the Manta Diablo, all the old hatred came back. I jumped up and pulled my knife from its sheath. It was a sharp knife, but not one I would have chosen to fight the Manta Diablo. Now I know that there is no such knife in the world.

"We will kill him together," I shouted.

The Sevillano glanced at the knife and then at me and began to laugh. "With that you could not kill the manta's grandmother," he said. "Sit down and hold onto the rail. If the manta starts to dive, cut the rope. Or else you and the boat will go down with him. And remember this, mate, do not touch the pearl."

An instant later the Sevillano leaped. He landed upon the broad platform of the Manta Diablo's back, slipped to his knees and crawled forward to where the harpoon stood embedded. He grasped the shaft with one hand and with the other drew his knife.

I doubt that the Manta Diablo was aware of him, either when he leaped or when he crawled along its spine or later as he grasped the harpoon's shaft. For it swam steadily on, half in and half out of the water, the pitch-black fins rising and falling without a change.

With all the strength of his powerful body, the Sevillano plunged the knife deep into the monster's neck, until it would go no farther. A tremor ran through the Manta Diablo and he rose out of the sea and fell back and his tail lashed the air over my head.

At a second thrust of the blade, as small waves streaked with blood washed across his back, the Manta Diablo struck the sea with his tail and a dull groan came from deep within him. He raised his fins over his back, as if to brush the Sevillano away. Then he dived and the rope snapped tight and the boat shot forward, spilling all the provisions into the sea.

I had not the least chance to cut the rope, as I had been told to do, in the brief moment before the sea-beast disappeared from sight.

At once, the boat moved sidewise and dipped forward and the bow scooped up a wave. All in a breath, we were going under when the rope began to fray, then hung by a thread and broke.

The Sevillano was on his knees. In his hands he held the harpoon. It could have been that he meant to drive the steel barb deeper, but while he knelt there and bloody spray almost hid him from my view, the end of the parted rope flew forward and wrapped around him, as a rope wraps around a maypole when children set it free.

Not a word came from the Sevillano nor a cry. His back was turned toward me and for a moment I glimpsed the tattoo he was proudest of, the picture across his wide shoulders in red and green and black of him killing the twelve-armed octopus. Then he went down with his sounding enemy, still with the harpoon grasped in his hands.

I righted the boat and after a time found the drifting oars and rowed back and forth over the place where the Sevillano had disappeared. The only thing I saw was a patch of foam and floating in it his cork-handled knife, the blade pointing downward.

At sunset I raised the sail and set a course toward La Paz. Only then did I think of the pearl. It lay in the bow of the boat where the Sevillano had put it, the one thing of all the things that had not been thrown into the sea.

18

The town was asleep when I sailed into the harbor, but cocks were crowing and there was not much time left before sunrise.

I pulled the boat up the shore and took off my shoes and tied the laces and hung the shoes around my neck. In my bare feet I walked softly along the Malecón so as not to disturb the stray dogs that sleep there under the trees, or the homeless who sleep in the doorways, and up the hill by a roundabout way. As I crossed the plaza the first light of morning shone on the church tower and its big bells.

The door creaked loudly when I opened it and I waited in the shadows until I was sure that no one had heard the sound.

A wooden screen stands just inside the door of our church where announcements are pinned up for people to read. In the center of the screen was a large sign, larger than any of the others, which offered a thousand pesos for the arrest of the thief who had stolen the Madonna's pearl. I took the sign down and put it in my pocket.

The church was deserted and only a few candles burned at the altar.

I walked down the aisle to the niche that was shaped like a shell, where the Madonna-of-the-Sea stood dressed in Her white gown and Her hair bound in a garland of flowers. The sweet smile was still on Her face and Her hand was held out to all sinners, whoever they were, even to me.

In Her hand I placed the great black pearl. "This now is a gift of adoration," I said, "a gift of love."

I then said a prayer for the soul of the Sevillano and one for my own. I also said a prayer for the Manta Diablo, that creature of beauty and of evil whom only two have seen with their eyes, though there are many who say they have and whom everyone in this life at sometime comes to know.

After my prayers I went quickly up the aisle. As I came to the door I stopped and turned back and climbed the long flight of steps that leads to the belfry and its three bronze bells.

The town lay below me. Women and sleepy children were on their way to the fountain with empty jars on their heads. The first blue smoke was rising from the chimneys everywhere. And across the plaza I could see one of the Indian girls sweeping the cobblestones in front of our big gate. It was Luz, whose husband had been drowned with the fleet at Punta Maldonado.

Beside me hung the big bells. I pulled hard on the rope and set them to swinging. It was yet an hour before the first service, so as the bells boomed out, people came running from the houses, to learn the reason for the alarm.

I untied my shoes and put them on and gave the rope another hard pull. By the time I reached the bottom of the stairs the church was crowded, so it was easy for me to slip away unnoticed.

Outside, the sun now lay golden on the roof tops and the big bells were still ringing over the town.

They rang in my heart, also, for this new day was the beginning day of manhood. It was not the day I became a partner in the House of Salazar nor the day I found the Pearl of Heaven. It was this day.

But as I walked homeward in the golden sun and the sound of bells hung in the air, I tried to think of a story to tell my mother. For she would not believe what had happened, any more than I believed the story she had told me long ago.

Turn the page for a special preview
of the

1996 NEWBERY HONOR BOOK

(ISBN 0-385-32175-9)

Enter the hilarious world of ten-year-old Kenny and his
family, the Weird Watsons of Flint, Michigan. There's
Momma, Dad, little sister Joetta, Kenny, and Byron, who's
thirteen and an "official juvenile delinquent." When Momma
and Dad decide it's time for a visit to Grandma, Dad comes
home with the amazing Ultra-Glide, and the Watsons set out
on a trip like no other. They're heading south. They're going
to Birmingham, Alabama, toward one of the darkest
moments in American history.

**Don't miss *The Watsons Go to Birmingham–1963*
by Christopher Paul Curtis.
On sale now from Delacorte Press!**

1. And You Wonder Why We Get Called the Weird Watsons

It was one of those super-duper-cold Saturdays. One of those days that when you breathed out your breath kind of hung frozen in the air like a hunk of smoke and you could walk along and look exactly like a train blowing out big, fat, white puffs of smoke.

It was so cold that if you were stupid enough to go outside your eyes would automatically blink a thousand times all by themselves, probably so the juice inside of them wouldn't freeze up. It was so cold that if you spit, the slob would be an ice cube before it hit the ground. It was about a zillion degrees below zero.

It was even cold inside our house. We put sweaters and hats and scarves and three pairs of socks on and still were cold. The thermostat was turned all the way up and the furnace was banging and sounding like it was about to blow up but it still felt like Jack Frost had moved in with us.

All of my family sat real close together on the couch under a blanket. Dad said this would generate a little heat but he didn't have to tell us this, it seemed like the cold automatically made us want to get together and huddle up. My little sister, Joetta, sat in the middle and all you could see were her eyes because she had a scarf wrapped around her head. I was next to her, and on the outside was my mother.

Momma was the only one who wasn't born in Flint so the cold was coldest to her. All you could see were her eyes too, and they were shooting bad looks at Dad. She always blamed him for bringing her all the way from Alabama to Michigan, a state she called a giant icebox. Dad was bundled up on the other side of Joey, trying to look at anything but Momma. Next to Dad, sitting with a little space between them, was my older brother, Byron.

Byron had just turned thirteen so he was officially a teenage juvenile delinquent and didn't think it was "cool" to touch anybody or let anyone touch him, even if it meant he froze to death. Byron had tucked the blanket between him and Dad down into the cushion of the couch to make sure he couldn't be touched.

Dad turned on the TV to try to make us forget how cold we were but all that did was get him in trouble. There was a special news report on Channel 12 telling about how bad the weather was and Dad groaned when the guy said, "If you think it's cold now, wait until tonight, the temperature is expected to drop into record-low territory, possibly reaching the negative twenties! In fact, we won't be seeing anything above zero for the next four to five days!" He was smiling when he said this but none of the Watson family thought it was funny. We all looked over at Dad. He just shook his head and pulled the blanket over his eyes.

Then the guy on TV said, "Here's a little something we can use to brighten our spirits and give us some hope for the future: The temperature in Atlanta, Georgia, is forecast to reach . . ." Dad coughed real loud and jumped off the couch to turn the TV off but we all heard the weatherman say, ". . . the mid-seventies!" The guy might as well have tied Dad to a tree and said, "Ready, aim, fire!"

"Atlanta!" Momma said. "That's a hundred and fifty miles from home!"

"Wilona . . . ," Dad said.

"I knew it," Momma said. "I knew I should have listened to Moses Henderson!"

"Who?" I asked.

Dad said, "Oh Lord, not that sorry story. You've got to let me tell about what happened with him."

Momma said, "There's not a whole lot to tell, just a story about a young girl who made a bad choice. But if you do tell it, make sure you get all the facts right."

We all huddled as close as we could get because we knew Dad was going to try to make us forget about being cold by cutting up. Me and Joey started smiling right away, and Byron tried to look cool and bored.

"Kids," Dad said, "I almost wasn't your father. You guys came real close to having a clown for a daddy named Hambone Henderson. . . ."

"Daniel Watson, you stop right there. You're the one

who started that 'Hambone' nonsense. Before you started that everyone called him his Christian name Moses. And he was a respectable boy too, he wasn't a clown at all."

"But the name stuck, didn't it? Hambone Henderson. Me and your granddaddy called him that because the boy had a head shaped just like a hambone, had more knots and bumps on his head than a dinosaur. So as you guys sit here giving me these dirty looks because it's a little chilly outside ask yourselves if you'd rather be a little cool or go through life being known as the Hambonettes."

Me and Joey cracked up, Byron kind of chuckled and Momma put her hand over her mouth. She did this whenever she was going to give a smile because she had a great big gap between her front teeth. If Momma thought something was funny, first you'd see her trying to keep her lips together to hide the gap, then, if the smile got to be too strong, you'd see the gap for a hot second before Momma's hand would come up to cover it, then she'd crack up too.

Laughing only encouraged Dad to cut up more, so when he saw the whole family thinking he was funny he really started putting on a show.

He stood in front of the TV. "Yup, Hambone Henderson proposed to your mother around the same time I did. Fought dirty too, told your momma a pack of lies about me and when she didn't believe them he told her a pack of lies about Flint."

Dad started talking Southern-style, imitating this

4

Hambone guy. "Wilona, I heard tell about the weather up that far north in Flint, Mitch-again, heard it's colder than inside a icebox. Seen a movie about it, think it was made in Flint. Movie called *Nanook of the North*. Yup, do believe for sure it was made in Flint. Uh-huh, Flint, Mitch-again.

"Folks there live in these things called igloos. According to what I seen in this here movie most the folks in Flint is Chinese. Don't believe I seen nan one colored person in the whole dang city. You a 'Bama gal, don't believe you'd be too happy living in no igloo. Ain't got nothing against 'em, but don't believe you'd be too happy living 'mongst a whole slew of Chinese folks. Don't believe you'd like the food. Only thing them Chinese folks in that movie et was whales and seals. Don't believe you'd like no whale meat. Don't taste a lick like chicken. Don't taste like pork at all."

Momma pulled her hand away from her mouth. "Daniel Watson, you are one lying man! Only thing you said that was true was that being in Flint is like living in a igloo. I knew I should have listened to Moses. Maybe these babies mighta been born with lumpy heads but at least they'da had *warm* lumpy heads!

"You know Birmingham is a good place, and I don't mean just the weather either. The life is slower, the people are friendlier—"

"Oh yeah," Dad interrupted, "they're a laugh a minute down there. Let's see, where was that 'Coloreds Only' bathroom downtown?"

"Daniel, you know what I mean, things aren't perfect

5

but people are more honest about the way they feel"—
she took her mean eyes off Dad and put them on Byron—"and folks there do know how to respect their
parents."

Byron rolled his eyes like he didn't care. All he did
was tuck the blanket farther into the couch's cushion.

Dad didn't like the direction the conversation was
going so he called the landlord for the hundredth time.
The phone was still busy.

"That snake in the grass has got his phone off the
hook. Well, it's going to be too cold to stay here tonight, let me call Cydney. She just had that new furnace
put in, maybe we can spend the night there." Aunt
Cydney was kind of mean but her house was always
warm so we kept our fingers crossed that she was home.

Everyone, even Byron, cheered when Dad got Aunt
Cydney and she told us to hurry over before we froze to
death.

Dad went out to try and get the Brown Bomber
started. That was what we called our car. It was a 1948
Plymouth that was dull brown and real big, Byron said it
was turd brown. Uncle Bud gave it to Dad when it was
thirteen years old and we'd had it for two years. Me and
Dad took real good care of it but some of the time it
didn't like to start up in the winter.

After five minutes Dad came back in huffing and
puffing and slapping his arms across his chest.

"Well, it was touch and go for a while, but the Great
Brown One pulled through again!" Everyone cheered,

but me and Byron quit cheering and started frowning right away. By the way Dad smiled at us we knew what was coming next. Dad pulled two ice scrapers out of his pocket and said, "O.K., boys, let's get out there and knock those windows out."

We moaned and groaned and put some more coats on and went outside to scrape the car's windows. I could tell by the way he was pouting that Byron was going to try and get out of doing his share of the work.

"I'm not going to do your part, Byron, you'd better do it and I'm not playing either."

"Shut up, punk."

I went over to the Brown Bomber's passenger side and started hacking away at the scab of ice that was all over the windows. I finished Momma's window and took a break. Scraping ice off of windows when it's that cold can kill you!

I didn't hear any sound coming from the other side of the car so I yelled out, "I'm serious, Byron, I'm not doing that side too, and I'm only going to do half the windshield, I don't care what you do to me." The windshield on the Bomber wasn't like the new 1963 cars, it had a big bar running down the middle of it, dividing it in half.

"Shut your stupid mouth, I got something more important to do right now."

I peeked around the back of the car to see what By was up to. The only thing he'd scraped off was the outside mirror and he was bending down to look at himself in it. He saw me and said, "You know what, square? I must be adopted, there just ain't no way two folks as ugly as your momma and daddy coulda give birth to someone as sharp as me!"

He was running his hands over his head like he was brushing his hair.

I said, "Forget you," and went back over to the other side of the car to finish the back window. I had half of the ice off when I had to stop again and catch my breath. I heard Byron mumble my name.

I said, "You think I'm stupid? It's not going to work this time." He mumbled my name again. It sounded like his mouth was full of something. I knew this was a trick, I knew this was going to be How to Survive a Blizzard, Part Two.

How to Survive a Blizzard, Part One had been last night when I was outside playing in the snow and Byron and his running buddy, Buphead, came walking by. Buphead has officially been a juvenile delinquent even longer than Byron.

"Say, kid," By had said, "you wanna learn somethin' that might save your stupid life one day?"

I should have known better, but I was bored and I think maybe the cold weather was making my brain slow, so I said, "What's that?"

"We gonna teach you how to survive a blizzard."

"How?"

Byron put his hands in front of his face and said, "This is the most important thing to remember, O.K.?"

"Why?"

"Well, first we gotta show you what it feels like to be trapped in a blizzard. You ready?" He whispered something to Buphead and they both laughed.

"I'm ready."

I should have known that the only reason Buphead and By would want to play with me was to do something mean.

"O.K.," By said, "first thing you gotta worry about is high winds."

Byron and Buphead each grabbed one of my arms and one of my legs and swung me between them going, "*Wooo,* blizzard warnings! Blizzard warnings! *Wooo!* Take cover!"

Buphead counted to three and on the third swing they let me go in the air. I landed headfirst in a snowbank.

But that was O.K. because I had on three coats, two sweaters, a T-shirt, three pairs of pants and four socks along with a scarf, a hat and a hood. These guys couldn't have hurt me if they'd thrown me off the Empire State Building!

After I climbed out of the snowbank they started laughing and so did I.

"Cool, Baby Bruh," By said, "you passed that part of the test with a B-plus, what you think, Buphead?"

Buphead said, "Yeah, I'd give the little punk a A."

They whispered some more and started laughing again.

"O.K.," By said, "second thing you gotta learn is how to keep your balance in a high wind. You gotta be good at this so you don't get blowed into no polar bear dens."

They put me in between them and started making me spin round and round, it seemed like they spun me for about half an hour. When slob started flying out of my mouth they let me stop and I wobbled around for a while before they pushed me back in the same snow-bank.

When everything stopped going in circles I got up and we all laughed again.

They whispered some more and then By said, "What you think, Buphead? He kept his balance a good long time, I'm gonna give him a A-minus."

"I ain't as hard a grader as you, I'ma give the little punk a double A-minus."

"O.K., Kenny, now the last part of Surviving a Blizzard, you ready?"

"Yup!"

"You passed the wind test and did real good on the balance test but now we gotta see if you ready to graduate. You remember what we told you was the most important part about survivin'?"

"Yup!"

"O.K., here we go. Buphead, tell him 'bout the final exam."

Buphead turned me around to look at him, putting my back to Byron. "O.K., square," he started, "I wanna make sure you ready for this one, you done so good so far I wanna make sure you don't blow it at graduation time. You think you ready?"

I nodded, getting ready to be thrown in the snowbank real hard this time. I made up my mind I wasn't going to cry or anything, I made up my mind that no matter how hard they threw me in that snow I was going to get up laughing.

"O.K.," Buphead said, "everything's cool, you 'member what your brother said about puttin' your hands up?"

"Like this?" I covered my face with my gloves.

"Yeah, that's it!" Buphead looked over my shoulder at Byron and then said, "*Wooo!* High winds, blowing snow! *Wooo!* Look out! Blizzard a-comin'! Death around the corner! Look out!"

Byron mumbled my name and I turned around to see why his voice sounded so funny. As soon as I looked at him Byron blasted me in the face with a mouthful of snow.

Man! It was hard to believe how much stuff By could put in his mouth! Him and Buphead just about died laughing as I stood there with snow and spit and ice dripping off of my face.

Byron caught his breath and said, "Aww, man, you flunked! You done so good, then you go and flunk the Blowin' Snow section of How to Survive a Blizzard, you forgot to put your hands up! What you say, Buphead, F?"

"Yeah, double F-minus!"

It was a good thing my face was numb from the cold

already or I might have froze to death. I was too embarrassed about getting tricked to tell on them so I went in the house and watched TV.

So as me and By scraped the ice off the Brown Bomber I wasn't going to get fooled again. I kept on chopping ice off the back window and ignored By's mumbling voice.

The next time I took a little rest Byron was still calling my name but sounding like he had something in his mouth. He was saying, "Keh-ee! Keh-ee! Hel' . . . hel' . . . !" When he started banging on the door of the car I went to take a peek at what was going on.

By was leaned over the outside mirror, looking at something in it real close. Big puffs of steam were coming out of the side of the mirror.

I picked up a big, hard chunk of ice to get ready for Byron's trick.

"Keh-ee! Keh-ee! Hel' me! Hel' me! Go geh Momma! Go geh Mom-ma! Huwwy uh!"

"I'm not playing, Byron! I'm not that stupid! You'd better start doing your side of the car or I'll tear you up with this iceball."

He banged his hand against the car harder and started stomping his feet. "Oh, please, Keh-ee! Hel' me, go geh Mom-ma!"

I raised the ice chunk over my head. "I'm not playing, By, you better get busy or I'm telling Dad."

I moved closer and when I got right next to him I could see boogers running out of his nose and tears running down his cheeks. These weren't tears from the cold either, these were big juicy crybaby tears! I dropped my ice chunk.

"By! What's wrong?"

"Hel' me! Keh-ee! Go geh hel'!"

I moved closer. I couldn't believe my eyes! Byron's mouth was frozen on the mirror! He was as stuck as a fly on flypaper!

I could have done a lot of stuff to him. If it had been me with my lips stuck on something like this he'd have tortured me for a couple of days before he got help. Not me, though, I nearly broke my neck trying to get into the house to rescue Byron.

As soon as I ran through the front door Momma, Dad and Joey all yelled, "Close that door!"

"Momma, quick! It's By! He's froze up outside!"

No one seemed too impressed.

I screamed, "Really! He's froze to the car! Help! He's crying!"

That shook them up. You could cut Byron's head off and he probably wouldn't cry.

"Kenneth Bernard Watson, what on earth are you talking about?"

"Momma, please hurry up!"

Momma, Dad and Joey threw on some extra coats and followed me to the Brown Bomber.

The fly was still stuck and buzzing. "Oh, Mom-ma! Hel' me! Geh me offa 'ere!"

"Oh my Lord!" Momma screamed, and I thought

she was going to do one of those movie-style faints, she even put her hand over her forehead and staggered back a little bit.

Joey, of course, started crying right along with Byron.

Dad was doing his best not to explode laughing. Big puffs of smoke were coming out of his nose and mouth as he tried to squeeze his laughs down. Finally he put his head on his arms and leaned against the car's hood and howled.

"Byron," Momma said, gently wiping tears off his cheeks with the end of her scarf, "it's O.K., sweetheart, how'd this happen?" She sounded like she was going to be crying in a minute herself.

Dad raised his head and said, "Why are you asking how it happened? Can't you tell, Wilona? This little knucklehead was kissing his reflection in the mirror and got his lips stuck!" Dad took a real deep breath. "Is your tongue stuck too?"

"No! Quit teasin', Da-ee! Hel'! Hel'!"

"Well, at least the boy hadn't gotten too passionate with himself!" Dad thought that was hilarious and put his head back on his arms.

Momma didn't see anything funny. "Daniel Watson! What are we gonna do?